Lincolnshire
COUNTY COUNCIL

discover libraries

JH

This book should be returned on or before the due date.

SAI

To renew or order library books please telephone 01522 782010
or visit https://lincolnshire.spydus.co.uk
You will require a Personal Identification Number.
Ask any member of staff for this.

The above does not apply to Reader's Group Collection Stock.

FmL.

"Stop thinking that you don't measure up somehow, because you're wrong."

Serafia gasped at his bold words. She couldn't hold back any longer. She lunged forward, pressing her lips against his before she lost her nerve. It had been a long time since she had trusted herself in all the various areas of her life, and romance had fallen to the bottom of the stack. What good was she to a man in the state she was in? Especially a prince? Still, she couldn't help herself.

And neither could Gabriel.

He met her kiss with equal enthusiasm. He held her face in his hands, drawing her closer and drinking her in. He groaned against her lips and then let his tongue slip along hers. His touch made her insides turn molten with need and wore away the last of her self-control.

At last, Gabriel pulled away, their rapid breaths hovering between them in the night air. "Is it too early to make our exit?" he asked.

Serafia shook her head and looked into his eyes. "I think the prince can leave whenever he wants to."

Seduced by the Spare Heir

ANDREA LAURENCE

MILLS & BOON

First published in Great Britain 2015
by Mills & Boon, an imprint of Harlequin (UK) Limited,
Large Print edition 2015
Eton House, 18-24 Paradise Road,
Richmond, Surrey, TW9 1SR

© 2015 Harlequin Books S.A.

Special thanks and acknowledgment are given to Andrea Laurence for her contribution to the *Dynasties: The Montoros* miniseries.

ISBN: 978-0-263-26041-0

Printed and bound in Great Britain
by CPI Antony Rowe, Chippenham, Wiltshire

ANDREA LAURENCE

is an award-winning author of contemporary romance for Mills & Boon® Desire and paranormal romance for Mills & Boon® Nocturne. She has been a lover of reading and writing stories since she learned to read at a young age. She always dreamed of seeing her work in print and is thrilled to share her special blend of sensuality and dry, sarcastic humor with the world.

A dedicated West Coast girl transplanted into the Deep South, Andrea is working on her own happily-ever-after with her boyfriend and their collection of animals, including a Siberian husky that sheds like nobody's business. If you enjoy Gabriel and Serafia's story, tell her by visiting her website, andrealaurence.com; like her fan page on Facebook at facebook.com/authorandrealaurence; or follow her on Twitter, twitter.com/andrea_laurence

To my fellow authors in the Montoros series—Janice, Katherine, Kat, Jules and Charlene.
It was a joy working with all of you. Thanks for tolerating my eighty million questions on the loop.

And to our editor, Charles— You're awesome, as always. I look forward to working with you again.

One

This party was lame. And it was *his* party. How could his own party be lame?

Normally parties were Gabriel Montoro's thing. Much to the chagrin of his family, he'd earned quite the reputation as "Good Time Gabriel." Music, alcohol, dim lighting, superficial conversation... He was the king of the party domain. But now that Gabriel had been tapped as the new king of Alma, everything had changed.

Gabriel gripped his flute of champagne and looked around the ballroom at his family's Coral Gables estate. Their tropical retreat seemed incredibly stuffy tonight. There wasn't a single flip-flop in the room, much less one of the feral parrots that lived on their property and flew in the occasional open door. His family had always had money, but they hadn't been pretentious.

But things had changed for the Montoro family since the tiny European island nation of Alma decided to restore their monarchy. Suddenly he was Prince Gabriel, third in line to the throne. And before he could adjust to the idea of that, his father and his older brother were taken out of the running. His parents had divorced without an annulment, making his father ineligible. Then, his ever-responsible brother abdicated and ran off with a bartender. Suddenly he was on the verge of being King Gabriel, and everyone expected him to change with the title.

This suffocating soiree was just the beginning and he knew it. Next, he'd have to trade in his South Beach penthouse for a foreign palace and his one-night stands for a queen with a pedigree. Everything from his clothes to his speech would be up for public critique by "his people." People he'd never seen, living on an island he'd only visited once. But his coronation was only a month or two away. He left for Alma in a week.

That was why they were having this party, if you could even call it that. The music was classical, the drinks were elegant and the women were wearing far too much clothing. He got a sinking feeling in his stomach when he realized this was how it was going to be from now on. Boring parties with boring people he didn't even know kissing his ass.

There were two hundred people in the room, but there were more strangers than anything else. He found that terribly ironic. People had come out of the woodwork since his brother, Rafe, abdicated and Gabriel was thrust into the spotlight. Suddenly he wasn't just the vice president of South American Operations, cast into the Southern Hemisphere where he couldn't embarrass the family; he was the hot ticket in town.

Him! Gabriel—the middle child whom no

one paid any attention to, the one dismissed by his family's society friends as the bad boy, the spare heir and nothing more. Now that he was about to be king, he had strangers at every turn fighting to be his new best friends.

He hated to break it to them, but Gabriel didn't have friends. Not real ones. That required a level of trust in other people that he just didn't have. He'd learned far too young that you can't trust anyone. Even family could let you down when you need them the most.

Speak of the devil.

From across the room, his cousin Juan Carlos spied him and started in his direction. He was frowning. Nothing new there. Ever serious, Juan Carlos never seemed to have any fun. He was always having business discussions, working, being responsible. He was the kind of man who should be the king of Alma—not Gabriel. After hundreds of years, why hadn't people figured out that bloodlines were not the best indicator of leadership potential?

"You're not talking to anyone," Juan Carlos

noted with a disapproving scowl as he loomed over his cousin. At several inches over six feet, he had a bad habit of hovering over people. Gabriel was never quite sure if his cousin deliberately tried to intimidate with his size or if he was unaware how much it bothered people when he did that.

Gabriel wasn't about to let his cousin's posture or his frown get to him. He tended not to worry too much about what his cousin thought, or what anyone thought, really. When it came down to it, Juan Carlos was serious enough for them both. "No one is talking to me," he corrected.

"That's because you're hiding in the corner sulking."

Gabriel scoffed at his blunt observation. "I am not sulking."

His cousin sighed and crossed his arms over his chest. "Then what would you call it?"

"Surveying my domain. That sounds kingly, right?"

Juan Carlos groaned and rolled his eyes. "Quit

it. Don't even pretend you care about any of this, because I know you don't. You and I both know you'd much rather be in South Beach tonight chasing tail. Pretending otherwise is insulting to your family and insulting to your country."

Gabriel would be lying if he said the neon lights weren't beckoning him. There was nothing like the surge of alcohol through his veins and the thumping bass of music as he pressed against a woman on the dance floor. It was the only thing that could help him forget what a mess he was in, but after the drama with Rafe, he'd been on a short leash. The family couldn't take another scandal.

That didn't mean he felt like apologizing for who he was. He wasn't raised to be king. The Alman dictatorship had held strong for nearly seventy years. Who would've thought that when democracy was restored, they'd want their old royal family back? They hadn't anticipated this summons and he certainly hadn't anticipated his brother, the rightful king, would run off with a Key West bartender and send Gabriel's life into a tailspin. "I'm sorry if that offends your sensibilities, J.C., but I didn't ask to be king."

"I know you didn't ask to be king. It is plainly obvious to every person in this room that you don't want the honor. But guess what? The crown has landed in your lap and you've got to step up and grow up." Juan Carlos sipped his wine and glared at Gabriel over the rim. "And what have I told you about calling me that?" he added.

That made Gabriel smile. Annoying his cousin was one of his favorite pastimes since child-hood. The smile was short-lived, though.

It wasn't the first time he'd been told to grow up. What his family failed to realize was that Gabriel had grown up a long time ago. They all liked to pretend it didn't happen, but in a dark room with thick rope cutting into his wrists, he'd left his childhood and innocence behind with his captors. If his family had wanted him to act responsibly, they should've done more to rescue him. He'd survived because of his own quick thinking and his first choice as an adult was to live the life he wanted and not care what anyone else thought about it.

Grow up, indeed. Gabriel took a large swallow of his champagne and sighed. The days of living his life as he chose were numbered. He could feel it. Soon it wouldn't just be his father and cousin trying to tell him what to do.

"Always good talking with you, cuz. Don't you have someone to schmooze?"

Juan Carlos didn't respond. Instead he turned on his heel and walked over to the dessert table. Within seconds, he was chatting with someone influential, whose name Gabriel had forgotten, over silver platters of chocolate truffles and cream puffs.

Gabriel turned away, noticing the side door that led out to the patio and garden pavilion. Hopefully he could make it out there before someone noticed.

Glancing around quickly, he spied his father with his back to him. His sister was chatting with a group of ladies in the corner. This was his chance. He moved toward the door and surged through it as fast as he could.

Gabriel was immediately rewarded with the oppressive wave of heat that July in Miami was known for. The humid blast hit him like a tsunami after the air-conditioned comfort of the ballroom, but he didn't care. He moved away from the door and out into the dark recesses of the patio.

There were some tables and chairs set up outside in case guests wanted to come out. They were draped with linens and topped with centerpieces of candles and roses. All the seats were empty. Gabriel was certain none of the ladies were interested in getting overheated in their fancy clothes with their meticulously styled hair and makeup.

Glancing over at the far end of the semicircular patio, he spied someone looking out into the gardens. The figure was tall, but slender, with the moonlight casting a silver silhouette that highlighted the bare shoulders and silk-hugging curves. She turned her head to watch a bird fly through the trees and he was rewarded with a glimpse of the cheekbones that had made her famous.

Serafia.

The realization sent a hot spike of need down his spine and the blood sped through his veins as his heart beat double-time. Serafia Espina was his childhood crush and the fantasy woman of every red-blooded man who had ever achieved puberty. Eight years ago, Serafia had been one of the biggest supermodels in the industry. Like all the greats, she'd been known by only her first name, strutting down catwalks in Paris, New York and Milan wearing all the finest designers' clothes.

And she'd looked damn good in them, too.

Gabriel didn't know much about what had happened, but for health reasons, Serafia had suddenly given up modeling and started her own business of some kind. But judging by the way that red dress clung to her curves, the years hadn't dulled her appeal. She could walk the catwalk right now and not miss a beat.

He hadn't spoken to Serafia in years. When his family was overthrown by the Tantaberras, they had fled to the United States and the Espinas moved to Switzerland. In the 1980s, they'd moved to Spain and their families renewed their friendship. When Gabriel and Serafia were children, their families vacationed together on the Spanish Riviera. Back then, he'd been a shy, quiet little boy of ten or eleven and she was the beautiful, unobtainable older woman. She was sixteen and he was invisible.

This was a fortunate encounter. They weren't children anymore and as the future king of their home country, he was anything but invisible. As Mel Brooks famously said, "It's good to be the king."

Serafia felt the familiar, niggling sensation of someone's eyes on her. It was something she'd become keenly attuned to working in the modeling business. Like a sixth sense, she could feel a gaze like a touch raking over her skin. Judging. Critiquing.

She turned to look behind her and found the man of the evening standing a few feet away. Gabriel had certainly grown up a lot since she saw him last. He was looking at her the way most men did—with unmasked desire. She supposed she should be flattered to catch the eye of the future king, but he was in his twenties, just a baby. He didn't need to get involved with an older, has-been model with enough baggage to pack for a long vacation.

"Your Majesty," she replied with a polite bow of her head.

Gabriel narrowed his gaze at her. "Are you being sarcastic?" he asked.

Serafia's mouth dropped open with surprise, her response momentarily stolen. That wasn't what she was expecting him to say. "Not at all. Did it come out that way? If it did, I sincerely apologize."

Gabriel shook his head dismissively and walked toward her. He didn't look like any king she'd ever seen before. He exuded a combination of beauty and danger, like a great white shark, gliding gracefully across the stone patio in a tailored black suit and dress shirt. His tie was bloodred and his gaze was fixed on her as if she were prey.

She felt her chest tighten as he came closer and she breathed in the scent of his cologne mingling with the warm smell of the garden's exotic flowers. Her fight-or-flight instincts were at the ready, even as she felt herself get drawn closer to him.

He didn't pounce. Instead he leaned down, rested his elbows on the concrete railing and looked out into the dark recesses of the tropical foliage. "It's not you, it's me," he said. "I still haven't quite adjusted to the idea of all this royalty nonsense."

Royalty nonsense. Wow. Serafia's libido was doused with cold water at his thoughtless words. That wasn't exactly what the people of Alma wanted to hear from their new king. After the collapse of the dictatorship, restoring the monarchy seemed like the best way to stabilize the country. The wealthy Alma elite would get a little more than they bargained for with Gabriel Montoro wearing the crown. He didn't really seem to care about Alma or the monarchy. He hadn't grown up there, but neither had she. Her parents had raised her to value her heritage and her homeland, regardless.

Perhaps it was just his youth. Serafia knew how hard it was to have the spotlight on you at such a young age. She'd been discovered by a modeling agency when she was only sixteen. Whisked away from her family, she was making six figures a year when most teenagers were just getting their driver's licenses. By the time she was old enough to drink, she was a household name. The pressure was suffocating, pushing her to her personal limits and very nearly destroying her. She couldn't even imagine what it would be like to be the ruler of a country and have over a million people depending on her.

"I think you'll get used to it pretty quickly," she said, leaning her hip against the stone railing. She picked up her glass of wine and took a sip. "All that power will go to your head in no time."

Gabriel's bitter laugh was unexpected. "I doubt that. While I may be king, my family will ensure that I'm not an embarrassment to them."

"I thought a king can do what he likes."

"If that was true, my father or my brother would still be in line for the crown. In the end, even a king has a mama to answer to." Gabriel looked at her with a charming smile, running his fingers through his too-long light brown hair.

It was shaggy and unkempt, a style popular with men his age, but decidedly unkingly. The moonlight highlighted the streaks of blond that he'd probably earned on the beach. She couldn't tell here in the dark, but from the pictures she'd seen of him in the papers and online, he had the tanned skin to match. Even in his immaculate and well-tailored suit, he looked more like a famous soccer player than a king.

"And I know your mama," she noted. Señora Adela was a beautiful and fierce woman who lived and loved with passion. She'd also been one to give the lecture of a lifetime while she pulled you down the hallway by your ear. "I'd behave if I were you."

"I'll try. So, how have you been?" he asked, shifting the conversation away from his situation. "I haven't seen you since you became a famous supermodel and forgot about all of us little people."

Serafia smiled, looking for the right answer. She knew people didn't really want to know how she was doing; they were just being polite. "I've been well. I started my own consulting business since I left modeling and the work has kept me fairly busy."

"What kind of consulting?"

"Image and etiquette, mostly. I traveled so extensively as a model that I found I could help companies branch out into unfamiliar foreign markets by teaching them the customs and societal norms of the new country. Other times I help wealthy families groom their daughters into elegant ladies."

Although families mostly paid her to teach etiquette and poise and give makeovers, she also spent a lot of time trying to teach those same girls that being pretty wasn't all they had to offer the world. It was an uphill battle and one that had earned her the label "hypocrite" more than a time or two. Sure, it was easy for a supermodel to say that beauty wasn't everything.

"Do me a favor and don't mention your consulting business around my father or Juan Carlos," Gabriel said.

Serafia's dark eyebrows knit together in confusion. "Why is that? Do they have daughters in need of a makeover?" Bella certainly didn't need any help from her. The youngest Montoro was looking lovely tonight in a beaded blue gown with her golden hair in elegantly twisted curls.

Serafia had heard rumors that the Montoro heirs had been allowed to run wild in America, but from what she had seen, they were no different from the youths of any other royal family. They wanted to have fun, find love and shirk their responsibilities every now and then. Until those desires interfered with the crown, as Rafe's abdication had, there was no harm done.

Gabriel shook his head and took a large sip of his champagne. "No daughters. They've just got *me*. I wouldn't be surprised if they'd jump at the chance to have you make me over. I don't really blame them. I'm about to be the most unsuitable king ever to sit upon the throne of Alma. The bad boy…the backup plan…the worst possible choice…"

Her eyes widened with every unpleasant description. "Is that their opinion or just your own?"

He shrugged. "I think it's everyone's opinion, including mine."

"I think you're exaggerating a little bit. I'm not sure about what your family thinks behind closed doors, but I haven't heard anything about you being unsuitable. Everyone is surprised about Rafe abdicating, of course, but I just came from Alma and the people are very excited to have you come home and serve as their monarch."

She hadn't originally planned on visiting Alma, but she'd gotten a call from a potential client there. She was already coming to Florida to consult with a company in Orlando, so she made a stop in Alma on the way. She was glad she had. It was inspiring to see an entire country buzzing with hope for the future. She wished she saw some of that same excitement in Gabriel.

He narrowed his gaze, seemingly searching her expression for the truth in her words, but he didn't appear to find it. "That won't last long. I wouldn't be surprised if they'd start begging for the dictatorship to come back within a year of my reign beginning."

And Serafia had thought she was the only one around here with miserably low self-esteem. "The people of Alma fought long and hard to be free of the Tantaberras. You would have to be a wicked, bloodthirsty tyrant for them to wish his return. Is that what you have planned? A reign of terror for your people?"

"No. I guess that changes things," he said with

a bright smile that seemed fake. "I didn't realize they had such low expectations for their king. As long as I don't decapitate all my enemies and force my subjects to cower in fear, I'll be a success! Thanks for letting me know that. I feel a lot better about the whole thing now."

Gabriel was leaving for Alma in a week, and that attitude was going to be a problem. Before she could curb her tongue, Serafia leaned in to him and plucked the champagne glass from his hand. "The citizens of Alma have been through a lot over the last seventy years. While the wealthy upper class could afford to flee, most of the people were trapped there to suffer at the hands of Tantaberra and his sons. They're finally free, some of them having waited their whole lives to wake up in the morning without the oppressive hand of a despot controlling them. These people have chosen to restore your family to the throne to help them rebuild Alma. They can probably do without your sarcasm and self-pity."

Gabriel looked at her with surprise lighting

his eyes. He might not be comfortable with the authority and responsibility of being king, but he seemed shocked that she would take that tone of voice with him. She didn't care. She had lived in Spain her whole life. She wasn't one of his subjects and she wasn't about to grovel at his feet when he was being like this.

She waited for him to speak, watching as the surprise faded to heat. At first she thought it was anger building up inside him, but when his gaze flicked over her skin, she could feel her cheeks start to burn with the flush of sexual awareness. She might have been too bold and said too much, but he seemed to like it for some reason.

At last, he took a deep breath and nodded. "You're absolutely right."

That was not what she'd expected to hear at all. She had braced herself for an argument or maybe even a come-on line to change the subject, but she certainly didn't think he would agree with her. Perhaps he wasn't doomed to failure if he could see reason in her words. She returned his glass of champagne and looked out into the garden to avoid his intense stare and hide her blush. "I apologize for being so blunt, but it needed to be said."

"No, please. Thank you. I have spent the days since my brother's announcement worried about how it will impact me and my life. I've never given full consideration to the lives of all the people in Alma and how they feel. They have suffered, miserably, for so long. They deserve a king they can be proud of. I'm just afraid I'm not that man."

"You can be," Serafia said, and as she spoke the words, she believed them. She had no real reason to be so certain about the success of the Montoro Bad Boy. She hadn't spoken to him in years and he was just a boy then. Now there were only the rumors she'd heard floating across the Atlantic—stories of womanizing, fast cars and dangerous living. But she felt the truth deep in her heart.

"It might take time and practice, but you can get there. A lesser man wouldn't give a second thought to whether he was the right person for the job. You're genuinely concerned and I think that bodes well for your future in Alma."

Gabriel looked at her and for the first time, she noticed the signs of strain lining his eyes. They didn't entirely mesh with the image that had been painted of the rebellious heir to the throne. He seemed adept at covering his worry with humor and charming smiles, but in that moment it all fell away to reveal a man genuinely concerned that he was going to fail his country. "Do you really believe that?"

Serafia reached out and covered his hand with her own. She felt a warm prickle dance across her palm as her skin touched his. The heat of it traveled up her arm, causing goose bumps to rise across her flesh despite the oppressive Miami summer heat. His gaze remained pinned on her own, an intensity there that made her wonder if he was feeling the same thing. She was startled by her reaction, losing the words of comfort she'd intended to say, but she couldn't pull away from him.

"Yes," she finally managed to say in a hoarse whisper.

He nodded, his jaw flexing as he seemed to consider her response. After a moment, he slipped his hand out from beneath hers. Instead of pulling away, he scooped up her hand in his, lifting it as though he was going to kiss her knuckles. Her breath caught in her throat, her tongue snaking out across her suddenly dry lips.

"Serafia, can I ask you something?"

She nodded, worried that she was about to agree to something she shouldn't, but powerless to stop herself in that moment. The candlelight flickering in his eyes was intoxicating. She could barely think, barely breathe when he touched her like that.

"Will you..." He hesitated. "...help me become the kind of king Alma deserves?"

Two

Gabriel watched as Serafia's expression collapsed for a moment in disappointment before she pulled herself back together. He couldn't understand why he saw those emotions in her dark eyes. He thought she would be excited that he wanted to step up and be a better person for the job. Wasn't that what she'd just lectured him about?

Then he looked down at her hand clutched in his own, here in the candlelight, on the dark, secluded patio, and realized he had a pretty solid seduction in progress without even trying. That might be the problem. He'd been too distracted by their conversation to realize it.

He had to admit he was pleased to know she responded to him. In the back of his mind, he'd considered Serafia unobtainable, a childhood fantasy. The moment she'd turned to look at him tonight, he felt his heart stutter in his chest as if he'd been shocked by a defibrillator. Her stunning red silk gown, rubies and diamonds dangling at her throat and ears, crimson lipstick against the flawless gold of her skin…it was as though she'd walked out of a magazine spread and onto his patio.

She was poised, elegant and untouchable. And bold. With a razor-sharp tongue, she'd cut him down to size, sending a surprising surge of desire through him instead of anger. She didn't care that he was the crown prince; she was going to tell it the way it was. With everything ahead of him, he was beginning to think he needed a woman like that in his life. Gabriel was already surrounded by too many yes-men or needling family members.

Serafia was a firecracker—beautiful, alluring and capable of burning him. A woman like that didn't exist in real life, and if she did, she wouldn't want anything to do with a man like Gabriel. Or so he'd always thought. The disappointment in her dark eyes led him to believe that perhaps he was wrong about that.

He wasn't entirely sure that a haircut and a new suit would make him a better king, but he was willing to give it a try. It certainly couldn't hurt. Working with a professional image consultant would get his father and Juan Carlos off his back. And if nothing else, it would keep this beautiful, sexy woman from disappearing from his life for at least two more weeks. It sounded like a win-win for Gabriel.

"A makeover?" she said after the initial shock seemed to fade from her face. She pulled her fingers from his grasp and rubbed her hands together for a moment as if to erase his touch. Serafia didn't seem to think his plan was the perfect solution he'd envisioned. "For you?"

"Why not? That's what you do, right?"

Her nose wrinkled and her brow furrowed. "I teach teenage girls how to walk in high heels and behave themselves in various social situations."

"How is what I'm proposing any different? Obviously I don't need the lesson on heels, but I'm about to face a lot of new social situations. With the way my family has been nagging at me, there seem to be a lot of land mines ahead of me. I could use help on how I should dress and what I should say. And I think you're the right person for the job."

Serafia's dark eyes widened and she sputtered for a moment as she struggled for words to argue with him. "I thought you didn't want a makeover," she said at last.

Gabriel crossed his arms over his chest. "I didn't want my family to force me into one. There's a difference. But you've convinced me that it's needed if I'm going to be the kind of king Alma needs."

"I don't know, Gabriel." She turned back to the gardens, avoiding his gaze. She seemed very hesitant to agree to it and he wasn't sure why. She'd pretty much dressed him down and chastised him for being a self-centered brat. Her words were bold and passionate. But then, when he asked for her help, she didn't want to be the one to change him. He didn't get it. Was he a lost cause?

"Come on, Serafia. It's perfect. I need a makeover, but I don't want everyone to know it. You're a friend of the family, so no one will think twice of you traveling with me or being seen with me. No one outside of the family even needs to know why you're here. We can come up with some cover story. I've got a week to prepare before I leave for Alma and another week of welcome activities once I arrive before things start to settle down. I'm not sure I can get through all that without help. Without *your* help."

"I can't just drop everything and run to your side, Gabriel."

"I'll pay you double."

She turned back to him, a crimson frown lining her face. Even that didn't make her classic features unattractive. "I don't need the money. I have plenty of that. I don't even have to work, but I was tired of sitting around with my own thoughts."

He wasn't sure what kind of thoughts would haunt a young, successful woman like Serafia, but he didn't feel that he should ask. "Donate it all to charity, then. I don't care. It's good for your business."

"How? I'd be doing this in secret. That won't earn me any exposure for my company."

"Not directly, but having you by my side in all the pictures will get your name in the papers. After you're seen with royalty, maybe your services will be more in demand because you have connections."

Serafia sighed. She was losing this battle and she knew it.

Gabriel looked at her, suppressing a smile as he prepared to turn her own argument against her and end the fight. "If for no other reason, do it for the people of Alma. You yourself just said how much these people have suffered. Do your part and help me be the best king I can possibly be."

She tensed up and started biting her lower lip. Picking up her wineglass, she took a sip and looked out at the moon hovering over the tree line. At last, her head dropped in defeat. The long, graceful line of her neck was exposed by the one-shoulder cut of her gown and the style of her hair. The dark, thick strands were twisted up into an elegant chignon, leaving her flawless, honey-colored skin exposed.

He wanted to press a kiss to the back of her neck and wrap his arms around her waist to comfort her. His lips tingled as he imagined doing just that, but he knew that would be pushing his luck. If she agreed to work with him over the next few weeks, there might be time for kisses and caresses later. It couldn't take every hour of the day to make him suitable. But if she left now, he'd never have the chance.

Taking a deep breath, she let it out and nodded. "Okay. We start tomorrow morning. I will be here at nine for breakfast and we'll begin with table manners."

"Nine?" He winced. Most Saturday mornings, he didn't crawl out of bed until closer to noon. Of course, he wouldn't be closing down the bars tonight. If he left the family compound, they'd likely release the hounds to track him down.

"Yes," she replied, her voice taking the same tone as the nuns had used when he was in Catholic school. Serafia didn't look a thing like Sister Mary Katherine, but she had the same focused expression on her face as she looked him over. The former supermodel had faded away and he was left in the presence of his new image consultant.

"Modern kings do not stay up until the wee hours of the morning and sleep until noon. They have a country to lead, meetings to attend and servants that need a reliable schedule to properly run the household. After breakfast, you're getting a haircut." She reached out for his hand, examining his fingernails in the dim lights. "And a manicure. I'll have someone come in to do it. If we went to a salon, people would start talking."

Getting up early, plus a haircut? Gabriel self-consciously ran his fingers through the long strands of his hair. He liked it long. When it was short, he looked too much like his toe-the-line brother, CEO extraordinaire Rafe. That wasn't him. He was VP of their South American division for a reason. Since the news of Alma's return to monarchy, he'd spent most of his time in Miami, but he preferred his time spent south of the equator. Life down there was more colorful, less regimented. He didn't even mind the constant threat of danger edging into his daily routine there. Once you'd been kidnapped, beaten and held for ransom, there wasn't much else to fear.

All that would end now. A new VP would take over South American Operations and Gabriel would take a jet to Alma. He'd be ruling over a country with a million citizens and dealing with all the demands that went with it.

What had he signed himself up for?

"I wish I had my tablet with me, but I'll just have to make all my notes when I get back to my hotel. Sunday, we're going through your wardrobe and determining what you can take with you to Alma. Monday morning, I'll arrange for a private shopper to come to the house and we'll fill in the gaps."

"Now, wait a minute," he complained, holding up his hands to halt her long list of tasks. He knew he could use some polishing, but it sounded as if Serafia was preparing to gut him and build him up from scratch. "What is wrong with my clothes? This is an expensive suit."

"I'm sure it is. And if you were the owner of an exclusive nightclub in South Beach, it would be perfect, but you are Prince Gabriel, soon to be King Gabriel."

He sighed. He certainly didn't feel like royalty. He felt like a little boy being scolded for doing everything wrong. But he'd brought this pain upon himself. Spending time with his fantasy woman hadn't exactly gone to plan. It had only been minutes since he made that decision and he was already starting to regret it.

"Are you dating anyone?"

Gabriel perked up. "Why? Are you interested?" he said with the brightest, most charming smile he could conjure.

Serafia wrinkled her nose at him and shook her head. "No. I was just wondering if I needed to work with you on dealing with any sticky romantic entanglements before you leave."

That was disappointing. "I'm not big on relationships," he explained. "There are plenty of women I've seen on and off, but there shouldn't be any heartbroken women trying to follow me to Alma."

"How about pregnant bartenders?" she asked pointedly.

Gabriel chuckled. His brother's relationship drama had everyone in the family on edge. If he didn't work out, the crown would be dumped on Bella and she was only twenty-three, barely out of college. "No pregnant bartenders that I am aware of," he answered. "Or dancers or cocktail waitresses or coeds. I'm extremely careful about that kind of thing."

"You always use protection? Every time?"

Gabriel stiffened. "Do we really have to talk about my sex life?"

Serafia sighed and shook her head. "You have no real idea what you've gotten yourself into, do you? From now on, your sex life is the business of a whole country. Who you're seeing and who might be your future queen will be one of the first issues you'll tackle as king. After that, fathering heirs and continuing the Montoro bloodline will be the chief concern of each of your subjects. Every woman you're seen with is a candidate for queen. Every time your wife turns down a glass of wine or puts on a few pounds, there will be pregnancy rumors. Privacy has gone out the window for you, Gabriel."

"There's not going to be someone in the room while I *father* these heirs, is there?"

At that, Serafia smiled. "No. They have to draw the line somewhere."

That offered little comfort to Gabriel in the

moment. Each step he took toward being king, the more concerned he became. He wanted to be a good leader, but the level of scrutiny in every aspect of his life was suffocating. His hair, his clothes, his sex life… He could feel the pressure crushing against his chest like a pile of stones.

Serafia pointed to a pair of chairs nearby. "Why don't we sit down for a minute. You look like you're about to pass out and these shoes are starting to pinch."

Gabriel pulled out a chair for her and took the one beside her. "I guess I just never thought about all this before. A few weeks ago, I was just a VP in my family company, someone with far-off ties to a country and a history most of us have forgotten all about. Then, boom, I'm a prince. And before I can adjust to that, I find out that I'm going to be king of the place. My life has taken a strange turn."

She nodded sympathetically. "I hate to be the one to tell you this, but it's just going to get worse. Once you're in the spotlight, your life is no longer your own. But from someone who's lived through it, know that the sooner you adjust to the idea of it, the better off you'll be."

Serafia hated to see Gabriel like this. He seemed like such a vibrant, fun-loving man, and the weight of his future was slowly crushing him like a bug. She was pushing him. Maybe more than she had to, at least at first, but he needed to know how things were going to be now. He would adjust to the crown much more easily if he understood the consequences of it.

"Is that what it was like for you? Is that why you gave up modeling?"

Serafia couldn't help the pained expression she felt crossing her face. It happened every time her old career came up. She smiled and shook her head. "That was just a part of it."

"Do you miss modeling?" he asked.

"Not at all," she said a touch too quickly, although she meant it. It wasn't the glamorous business everyone thought it was. It was harsh, and despite how many millions she made doing it and how famous she became, there were still days where she was treated like little more than a walking coat hanger. And a fat one at that. "I'm not really interested in being in the spotlight anymore. It is both a wonderful and terrifying place to live."

Gabriel nodded thoughtfully. "The runways and magazine covers suffer for your absence. I understand why you stopped after what happened to you on the runway, though. I can imagine it's scary to come that close to death without any kind of warning. I mean, to go all that time without knowing you had…what was it, exactly?"

"A congenital heart defect," she replied, the lie slipping effortlessly off her tongue after all these years.

"Yeah, that's terrifying to think your own body is just waiting to rebel against you."

Serafia stiffened and tried to nod in agreement. That would be frightening, although she really wouldn't know. Her parents had done an excellent job spreading misinformation about her very public heart attack. Why else would a perfectly healthy twenty-four-year-old woman go into cardiac failure on the runway and drop to the floor with a thousand witnesses standing by in horror?

She could think of a lot of reasons, and for her, all of them were self-inflicted. Serafia had fallen victim to an industry-endorsed eating disorder, which had spiraled out of control leading up to that day. Anorexia was a serious illness, an issue that needed more visibility in the cut-throat modeling industry, but her family wanted to keep the truth out of the papers for her own protection. At the time, she had been in no condition to argue with them on that point.

Instead the word was that she'd retired from the modeling business to get treatment for her "heart condition" and no one ever questioned it. Instead of surgeries, her actual treatment had included nearly a year of intensive rehabilitation. She had to slowly put on thirty pounds so she didn't strain her heart. Then she learned to eat properly, how to exercise correctly and most important how to recognize the signs in herself that she was slipping into bad habits again.

"Are you better now?" he asked.

That was debatable. With an eating disorder, every day was a challenge. It wasn't like being an alcoholic or a drug user, where you could avoid the substance of choice. She had to eat. Every day. She needed to exercise. Just not too much. She had to maintain her weight and not swing wildly one way or another, or she'd put too much strain on her damaged heart. But she was managing. One day at a time, she reminded herself. "Yes," she said instead. "The doctors got me all fixed up. But you're right, I couldn't face the catwalk again after that. After nearly dying, I realized I wanted to do something else with my life. I'm much happier with what I'm doing now."

"Gabriel Alejandro Montoro!" a sharp voice shouted through the doorway to the patio. It was followed by several loud steps across the stone and a moment later, the figure of his younger sister, Bella, appeared.

"There you are. Everyone has been looking for you."

Gabriel shrugged, unaffected by his sister's exasperation. "I've been right here the whole time. And since when do you get to call me by my full name? Only Mama gets to do that."

"And if Mama were here, she'd haul you back into the house by your ear."

Serafia chuckled. Her memories of Adela were spot-on. "I'm sorry to monopolize Gabriel's time," she said, hoping to draw down some of his sister's ire. "We were discussing the plans for his royal transformation."

Bella eyed Serafia suspiciously, then turned to look at Gabriel. "Good luck with that. Either way, Father wants you inside, and now. He's wanting to do some kind of toast and then he wants to see you out on the dance floor. The press wants a shot of you dancing."

Gabriel stood with a reluctant sigh, reaching out his hand to help Serafia up. "And so it begins. Would you care to join me inside?"

"Absolutely." Serafia slipped her arm through his and they walked back into the house together.

There were even more people in the room now than there were when she'd decided it was too crowded and gone outside. Nothing she could do about it, though. She stayed by his side as they cut through the crowd in search of his father. They found him standing by the bar with Gabriel's cousin, Juan Carlos.

Serafia had never had much contact with the Salazar branch of the Montoro family, but she had heard good things about Juan Carlos. He had a good head on his shoulders. He was responsible and thoughtful. To hear some people talk, he was Gabriel's polar opposite and a better choice for king. She would never tell Gabriel that, though; he had enough worries. Perhaps Juan Carlos would accept a post as the king's counsel. He would make an excellent adviser for Gabriel or royal liaison to Alma's prime minister.

"There you are," Rafael said once he spied them. "Where have you..." He paused when his gaze flicked over Serafia. "Ah. Never mind. Now I know what has occupied your time," he said with a smile.

"It's good to see you again," she said, returning his grin and leaning in to hug her father's oldest friend.

"Too long!" Rafael exclaimed. "But now that some of us will be back in Alma, that will not be the case. Your father tells me he's considering moving back if the monarchy is stable."

"He told me that, as well." Her dad had mentioned it, but the Espina family was a little gun-shy when it came to their home country. Their quick departure from Alma in the 1940s had been a messy one. There were rumors and accusations thrown at anyone who fled before Tantaberra rose to power, and her family was not immune. Serafia knew they would move slowly on that front and some might never return. Spain was all she had ever known and she had fallen in love with Barcelona. It would take a lot to lure her away from her hacienda with beachfront views of the Mediterranean.

Rafael clapped his son on the back. "Now that you're here, I want to make a small speech, do a toast, and then maybe you can take a spin around the dance floor and encourage others to join you. The party is getting dull."

Gabriel nodded and Juan Carlos went over to silence the band and bring Rafael the microphone. The music stopped as Rafael stepped onto the riser with the band and raised his hand to get the crowd's attention. He had such a commanding presence; the whole room went deathly silent in a moment. He would've made a good king, too. Alma's archaic succession laws needed to be changed.

"Ladies and gentlemen," Rafael began. "I want to thank all of you for coming here tonight. Our family has waited seventy years for a night like this, when we could finally see the monarchy restored to Alma. With it, we hope to see peace, prosperity and hope restored for the people of Alma, as well. I'm thrilled to be able to stand up here and join all of you in wishing my son and future king, Prince Gabriel, all the success in the world as he returns to our homeland."

Several of the people in the crowd cheered and applauded Rafael's statement. Gabriel stood stiff at Serafia's side, his jaw tight and his muscles tense. He didn't seem to be as excited as everyone else. After their discussion outside, she understood his hesitation. Still clinging to his arm, she squeezed it reassuringly and smiled at him.

"I ask everyone here to raise their glass to the future king of Alma, Gabriel the First! Long live the king!"

"Long live the king!" everyone shouted as they held up their glasses and took a sip. Serafia raised her glass as well, drinking the last of her wine.

"Now I would like to ask Gabriel to step out onto the dance floor and show us a few moves. Everyone, please, join us."

"Looks like I have to ask a lady to join me on the dance floor." Gabriel leaned in closer to her, a sly smile curling his full lips. "Have your doctors cleared you for vigorous physical activity?"

Serafia smiled at Gabriel and nodded. "Oh yes, I've got a clean bill of health. I could go all night on the dance floor if you can keep up with me."

Gabriel took her hand and led her out into the center of the room. As the band started playing an upbeat salsa tune, his hand went to her waist and tugged her body tight against his. "Is that a challenge?" he asked.

The contact of his hard body against hers sent a shock wave through her system that she had little time to recover from. He was no longer the mop-topped little boy she remembered running up and down the beach with his kite. Now his green eyes glittered with attraction and a flash of danger. And he *was* dangerous. She might not have finished high school, but she read enough history to know that getting involved with a king never ended well.

Before she could answer him they started moving in time with the music. It had been a long time since she'd danced, but the movement came easily with his strong lead. She almost seemed to float across the wooden floors, the rhythm of the music pulsing through their bodies. The crowds and the cameras around them faded away as they moved as one.

Soon other couples joined them on the dance floor and she didn't feel so exposed. The people around her made her feel better about the prying eyes, but being in Gabriel's arms was still a precarious place to be. The way he held her, the way he looked at her… The next two weeks were going to be a challenge to her patience and her self-control. Gabriel wanted more from her than just a makeover, and when he held her, she felt the same way. She never should've accepted the job, and she knew that now.

This was no teenage girl or Spanish businessman she was dealing with here. Gabriel Montoro was a sexy, rebellious handful and if she wasn't careful, she was going to get in way over her head.

Three

"You're late. Again."

That wasn't anything Gabriel didn't already know. After the last few days he'd had, he wasn't really in the mood to hear it. He'd signed himself up for this nightmare, but he was almost to the point where he'd pay Serafia more to leave him alone than to stay. He was used to the constant criticism of his family, but for whatever reason, Serafia's critical comments grated on him. He just didn't want a woman like her pointing out his faults. He wanted her nibbling on his ear. Unfortunately critiquing him was her job.

"Thanks for the information," he snapped. "When I'm king, I will have you named the official court timekeeper."

He expected her to respond with a smart comment, but instead she turned on her heel and walked across the room. She returned a moment later with a velvet-covered tray in her hands. Laid across it were four different styles of watches.

"One of these, actually, will be the official court timekeeper. I had them brought over from a local jeweler for you to choose the one you like."

His cell phone chimed and he looked down at the screen to avoid the display of watches in front of him. It was a text from a woman he'd gone out with a few weeks ago: a brunette named Carla. He opted to ignore it. He'd been getting a lot of those texts lately and he couldn't do anything about them now that he was on house arrest. What would he say, anyway? "Sorry, love, I've got to fly to a country you've never heard of and be king"?

Slipping the phone back into his pocket, he sighed when he realized the tray of watches was still there, waiting on him. *Watches*. Gabriel hated watches. He didn't wear one, ever. And why did he need to with the clock on his cell phone? "I don't need a watch."

Her resolve didn't waver. "You say that, and yet I've noticed punctuality seems to be a problem for you."

Was she an image consultant or a drill sergeant? "It's not a problem for me. I'm fine. It seems to be more of a problem for you."

Serafia's pink lips tightened as she seemed to fight a frown. "Please choose one."

"I told you, I'm not going to wear a watch." Gabriel couldn't stand the feel of something on his wrists. He'd worn watches all through high school and college, but after his abduction, he gave them all away. Even the nicest watches reminded him of the restraints he'd worn for too long. In an instant, he was back in that cold, dark basement and he never ever wanted to go back to that place.

"There's a Ferragamo, a Patek Philippe and two Rolexes. How can you turn your nose up at a Rolex?" Serafia reached down and plucked one off the tray. "Try this on. It's steel and yellow gold, so it will coordinate nicely with whatever you might be wearing. The faceplate is surrounded by pave diamonds and there are diamonds on the hours. I think it will really look elegant—"

Gabriel didn't move fast enough and before he knew what she had planned, he felt the cold steel of the metal at his wrist. His whole body tensed in an instant. On reflex, he hissed and jerked away from her. He was instantly transported back to Venezuela and the dark, claustrophobic room he was held in for almost a week. He could smell the mildew and filth, the air stale and thick with humidity.

"I said no!" he shouted without intending to. His eyes flew open, taking in the open, airy bedroom. He drew in a deep breath of air scented with hibiscus flowers and felt the tension fade from his shoulders. Looking at Serafia, he immediately regretted his reaction. There was fear as real as his own reflected in her dark eyes. "I'm sorry to yell," he said, but it was too late. The damage was done.

She shied away from him, turning her back and carrying the hundred thousand dollars' worth of watches back to the desk. She didn't speak again until she returned, more composed. It was amazing how she always seemed so put together. He could rattle her for a moment, but she always seemed to snap right back. That was one skill he could use, but she hadn't taught him that yet.

She crossed her arms over her chest and looked at him. "What was all that about?"

Gabriel didn't like talking about his abduction. And his family had done a good job keeping the story out of the media. "I...I just don't like to wear a watch. I don't like the feel of anything around my wrists." He didn't want to elaborate. She already looked at him as if he was flawed. She had no idea how truly flawed he was. He was broken.

Serafia sighed, searching his face for answers he wasn't going to give her. "Okay, fine. No watch." She picked up her tablet and tapped through a few screens. "Your first public event in Alma will be a party hosted by Patrick Rowling. We need to get you fitted for your formal attire."

Patrick Rowling. Gabriel had heard his father and brother talking about the man, but he hadn't paid any attention. "Who is Patrick Rowling?"

"He's one of the richest men in Alma. He's British, actually, but when oil was discovered in Alma, his drilling company led the charge. He owns and operates almost all the oil platforms and refineries in the country. He's a very powerful and influential man. This party will be your first introduction to Alman society. Forging a solid relationship with the Rowlings will help secure a strong foothold for the monarchy."

Gabriel would be king, but somehow he got the feeling that he would be the one kissing Patrick's ring and not the other way around. He was already dreading this party and he didn't know anything about it.

"Now, this is a formal event, so custom dictates that you should wear ceremonial dress."

Serafia swung open the door of the armoire and pulled out a navy military uniform that looked like something out of an old oil painting in a museum. It looked stiff and itchy and he had absolutely no interest in wearing it.

"All right, now," he complained. "I've been a really good sport about most of this makeover stuff, but this is going too far." Gabriel frowned at Serafia as she held up the ridiculous-looking suit. "I let you cut my hair, give me a facial, a manicure, a pedicure and all other kinds of cures. You've given half my wardrobe to charity and spent thousands of dollars of my own money on suits no man under sixty would want to wear. I've tried to keep my mouth shut and go with it. But that...that outfit is ridiculous."

Serafia's eyes grew wider the longer he complained. "It's the ceremonial dress of the king!" she argued.

Of course it was. "It's got ropes and tassels and a damn baby-blue sash. I'm going to look like Prince Charming at the ball."

Serafia frowned. "That's the point, Gabriel. You are going to be *Su Majestad el Rey Don Gabriel I*. That's what kings wear."

"Maybe in the 1940s when my great-grand-father was the king. It's old-fashioned. Out-dated."

"It's not for every day. It's for events like coronations, weddings and formal events like this party at the Rowling Estate. The rest of the time you'll wear normal clothes."

"Normal clothes you picked out," he noted. Not much better in his estimation.

Serafia sighed and returned the suit to the armoire. When she shut the door, she slumped against it in a posture of defeat. Closing her eyes, she pinched the bridge of her nose between her fingers. "We leave for Alma in two days and we have so much to cover. At this rate, we're never going to get it all done. You hired me, Gabriel. Why are you fighting me on every little thing?"

He didn't think he was fighting her on everything. The watch issue was nonnegotiable, but they'd gotten that unpleasantness out of the way. The clothing was just a hard pill for him to swallow. "I'm not intentionally trying to make your job more difficult. It just seems to be a gift I have."

Serafia rolled her eyes. "So it seems. Admittedly, you appear to enjoy getting me all spun up. I've seen you smile through my irritation."

Gabriel had to admit that was true. There was something about the flush of irritation that made Serafia even that much more beautiful, if it was possible. In his mind, he imagined the same would hold true when she was screaming out in passion, clawing at the sheets. The woman who had sashayed down the runway all those years ago had nothing on the vision in his mind as he thought of her at night.

And he had. Since the night on the patio, he'd lain alone in bed every night thinking about her.

He hadn't intended to. Serafia was a fantasy from his younger years; the image of her in a bikini was the background of his first computer. It had been a long time since he'd had a crush on Serafia, and yet those desires had rushed back at the first sight of her.

It was probably his family-imposed curfew. The day his brother abdicated, he was practically dragged from his penthouse to the family compound. He'd gone weeks with no clubs, no bars, no socializing with friends at parties. His every move was watched and that meant he was on the verge of his longest dry spell since he broke the seal on his manhood.

It didn't really matter, though, at least where Serafia was concerned. He could've bedded a woman this morning and he would still want her the way he always had wanted her.

"Yes," he admitted at last. "I get pleasure from watching you spin."

"Why? Are you a sadist?"

Gabriel smiled wide and took a few steps closer to her. "Not at all. It might be cliché to say it, but, Serafia, you are even more beautiful when you're angry."

Serafia rejected the flicker of disbelief in the back of her mind and silenced the denial on her lips. As her therapist had trained her, she identified the negative thoughts and reframed them. She was a healthy, attractive woman. Gabriel found her eye-catching and it wasn't her place to question his opinion of her. "Thank you," she said. "But please don't spend the rest of our time together trying to annoy me. You might find I'm more attractive, but it's emotionally exhausting."

Gabriel took another step toward her, closing in on her personal space. With her back pressed against the oak armoire, she had no place to go or escape. A part of her didn't really want to escape, anyway. Not when he looked at her like that.

His dark green eyes pinned her in place, and her breath froze in her lungs. He wasn't just trying to flatter her with his words. He did want her. It was very obvious. But it wasn't going to happen for an abundance of reasons that started with his being the future king and ended with his being a notorious playboy. Even dismissing everything in between, it was a bad idea. Serafia had no interest in kings or playboys.

"Well, I'll do my best, but I do so enjoy the flush of rose across your cheeks and the sparkle of emotion in your dark eyes. My gaze is drawn to the tension along the line of your graceful neck and the rise and fall of your breasts as you breathe harder." He took another step closer. Now he could touch her if he chose. "If you don't want me to make you angry anymore, I could think of another way to get the same reaction that would be more...*pleasurable* for us both."

Serafia couldn't help the soft gasp that escaped her lips at his bold words. For a moment, she wanted to reach out for him and pull him hard against her. Every nerve in her body was buzzing from his closeness to her. She could feel the heat of his body radiating through the thin silk of her blouse. Her skin flushed and tightened in response.

One palm reached out and made contact with the polished oak at her back. He leaned in and his cologne—one of the few things she hadn't changed—teased at her nose with sandalwood and leather. The combination was intoxicating and dangerous. She could feel herself slipping into an abyss she had no business in. She needed to stop this before it went too far. Serafia was first and foremost a professional.

"I'm not sleeping with you," she blurted out.

Gabriel's mouth dropped open in mock outrage. "Miss Espina, I'm shocked."

Serafia chuckled softly, the laughter her only release for everything building up inside her. She arched one eyebrow at him. "Shocked that I would be so blunt or shocked that I'm turning you down?"

At that, he smiled and she felt her knees start to soften beneath her. Much more of that and she'd be a puddle in her Manolos.

"Shocked that you would think that was all I wanted from you."

Serafia crossed her arms over her chest. She barely had room for the movement with Gabriel so close. She needed the barrier. She didn't believe a word he said. "What exactly were you suggesting, then?"

His jewel-green gaze dropped down to the cleavage her movement had enhanced. She was clutching herself so tightly that she was on the verge of spilling out of her top. She relaxed, removing some, if not all of the distraction.

"I'm feeling a little caged up. I was going to suggest a jog around the compound followed by a dip in the swimming pool," he said.

"Sure you were," she replied with a disbelieving tone. "You look like a man who's hard up for a good run."

He smiled and she felt a part deep inside her clench with need. Desire had not been very high on Serafia's priority list for a very long time. She was frustrated at how easily Gabriel could push her body's needs to the top of the list.

"The king's health and well-being should be at the forefront of the minds of the Alman people. Long live the king, right?"

"Long live the king," she responded, albeit unenthusiastically.

"So, how about that run?"

The way he looked at her, the way he leaned into her, it felt as if he was asking for more than just a run. But she answered the question at hand and tried to ignore her body's response to his query. "First, you need your ceremonial dress tailored. It will take a couple days to get it back and we need it before we leave. Then you can run if you like."

"And what about you? Don't you need a little rush of endorphins? A little...release?"

"I exercised when I got up this morning," she replied. And she had. Every morning when she woke up, she did exactly forty-five minutes on her elliptical machine. No more, no less, doctor's orders. Her treadmill at home was gathering dust, since running was out of the question unless her life was in danger.

His gaze raked over her, making every inch of her body aware of his heavy appraisal before he made a sucking sound with his tongue and shook his head. "Pity."

He dropped his arm and took a step back, allowing her lungs to fill with fresh oxygen that wasn't tainted with his scent. It helped clear her head of the fog that had settled in when he was so close.

The persistent chirp of his cell phone drew his attention away and for that, Serafia was grateful. Apparently Gabriel's harem of women were lonely without him. Since they'd begun this process four days ago, he averaged a text or two an hour. Most of the time he didn't respond, but that didn't stop the messages from coming in. She didn't care about what he'd been involved in, but she couldn't help noticing all the different names on the screen.

Carla, Francesca, Kimi, Ronnie, Anita, Lisa, Tammy, Jessica, Emily, Sara...it was as if his phone was spinning through a massive Rolodex of names. His little digital black book would be ungainly if it were in print.

"I'm going to go see if the tailor has arrived," she said as he put the phone away again. "Do you think you can fight off all your lovers long enough to get this jacket fitted properly?"

Gabriel narrowed his eyes at her and slipped his phone into his pocket. "You sound jealous."

Maybe a little. But that was none of his concern. She would deal with it accordingly. "Not jealous," she corrected. "I'm concerned."

He frowned at her then. "You sound like my father. Why would you be concerned with my love life?"

"It's like I told you that first night, Gabriel. Your life is no longer your own. Not your relationships or your free time or even your body. You can't drive your sports cars around like a Formula One driver and put the king's health at risk. You can't party every night with a different woman and put the future of your country in the hands of a bastard you father with some girl you barely remember. You can't waste the realm's money on the hedonistic pleasures you've built your whole life on."

"From what I learned in school, that's what most kings do, actually."

"Maybe four hundred years ago, but not anymore. If King Henry the Eighth had to deal with the modern press, things would've ended very differently for him and all his poor wives."

"So you're saying it's all about appearances? I have to be squeaky clean on the outside to keep the press and the people happy?"

"It's bigger than that. Your recklessness is indicative of an emotional disconnect. That's what worries me. You need to prepare yourself for the marriage that is just around the corner for you. You may not even have met the woman yet, but I guarantee you'll be married before the first year of your reign comes to an end. That means no more skirt chasing. You have to take this seriously. You have to really connect with someone, and I don't see that coming easily to you."

"You don't think I can connect with someone?" He seemed insulted by her insinuation.

"Relationships—*real relationships*—are hard. Love and trust and honesty are difficult to maintain. I've only been around here for a few days, but I haven't seen you interact with a single person on a sincere level. You have no real relationships, not even with your family."

"I have real relationships," he argued, but even as he spoke the words, she sensed a question in his voice.

"Name one. If something huge happened in your life, who would you run to with the news? If you had a secret, who would you confide in?"

There was an extended silence as he thought about the answer to her question. There would be a quicker response for almost anyone else she asked this question of. A mother, a brother, a best friend, a buddy from college…Gabriel had no answer. It was both sad and disconcerting. Why did he keep everyone at arm's length?

"I have plenty of friends and family. Since I've been announced as the future king, they've been coming out of the woodwork. I don't know what you're talking about."

"I'm talking about having a person in your life who you can tell anything, good or bad. Someone to confide in. I don't think Jessica or Tammy is the right answer. But I also don't think Rafe or Bella are, either. Everyone needs a person like that in their lives. I feel like there are people who would be there for you, but you won't let them in. I feel a resistance, a buffer there, even with your own family, and I don't know what it's about. What I do know is that you need to learn to let those walls down or this week will be nothing compared to the next year."

"I figured the opposite would be true," he replied at last. "When you're the king, everyone wants something from you. You can't trust anyone. Your marriage is arranged, your closest advisers jockeying for their own pet projects. I would've thought that keeping my distance would be an asset in that kind of environment."

"Maybe you're right," she admitted with a sad shrug. "I certainly would've been more prepared for the world of modeling if I'd gone in believing that everyone wanted something from me and that I couldn't trust them. But I think everyone, even a king, needs someone."

"Believe me, it's easier this way," he said. "If you don't trust anyone, they can't betray you and you'll never be disappointed."

There was an honesty in his words that she hadn't heard in anything else he'd said when they were together. That worried her. Someone, at some point, had damaged Gabriel. She knew it shouldn't be her concern, but she couldn't help wondering what had happened and how she could help.

The people of Alma—Serafia included— wanted more from their king than Gabriel was willing to give them. He hadn't even been crowned king yet and she worried this was going to be a mistake. No amount of haircuts or fancy clothes could fix the break deep inside of him.

He had to do that himself.

Four

Two days later, Gabriel stepped onto a private jet and left the life he knew behind him. They flew overnight, his father, Rafael, sleeping in the bedroom of the plane as he and Serafia slept in fully reclining leather chairs. It was a quiet flight without a lot of conversation once they finished their dinners and dimmed the cabin lights.

Gabriel slept soundly, and when he awoke, they were thirty minutes out from landing in his new country. He'd only been there once before with Rafe on a whirlwind tour, but when he got off the plane this time, he was supposed to be their leader.

"You need to get dressed," Serafia said beside him. "Your suit is hanging up in the bathroom."

He hadn't heard her get up, but she had changed her clothes, refreshed her makeup and styled her thick, dark hair into a bun. For the next week, she was publically filling the role of his social secretary while privately coaching him through all the events. She was dressed for the part in a ladies' taupe suit. The blazer was well tailored and didn't look boxy, and the sheath dress beneath it was fitted and came down just to her knee, showcasing her long and shapely calves.

It was elegant, but Gabriel found himself longing for the clingy red silk gown from their first night together. In this outfit, she completely faded into the background. He supposed that was the idea, but he didn't like it. Serafia might not care for the spotlight, but she was born to be in it.

He went to the bathroom, getting ready and

changing into the navy suit she'd hung out for him. She'd paired it with a lighter blue shirt and a plain blue tie. It was a sophisticated look, she'd argued, but it seemed boring to him. It made him want to wear crazy socks, but he wouldn't. She'd already laid out a pair of navy socks for him.

By the time he came back out, his father had emerged from the bedroom and the pilot was announcing their descent into Del Sol, the capital of Alma.

"The press will be waiting for you when we arrive. They've arranged for a carpet to be laid out and your royal guards will be there for crowd control. They've already secured the area and screened all the attendees. Your press secretary, Señor Vega, briefed everyone on appropriate questions, so things should go smoothly. I will exit the plane first and make sure everything is okay," Serafia explained. "Then Señor Montoro, and then you're last. Wait until the carpet is clear. Take your time so everyone can get their photos."

Gabriel nodded, taking in her constant stream of instructions as he had done all week. She was a font of information.

"Don't forget to smile. Wave. It should just be the press, so no need to greet anyone in the crowd. No speeches, no interviews. Just smile and wave."

The wheels of the jet touched down and suddenly everything became very real. Gabriel looked out the window. Beyond the airport, he could see the great rock hills that rose on the horizon, their gray stone peppered with evergreens. Closer to Del Sol was a smaller hill topped with some kind of ancient fortress. Climbing up the incline were whitewashed buildings clustered together with clay tile roofs.

Ahead, clear blue skies with palm trees led the way toward the beach. His last trip here with his brother had been all business, so he had no idea what kinds of beaches they had in Alma, but he prayed they were at least halfway as nice as the ones in Miami. He was already feeling pangs of homesickness.

The plane stopped and the engines turned off. The small crew unlocked and extended the staircase. Serafia gathered up her bag and her tablet. "Smile and wave," she said one last time before disappearing down the stairs.

His father followed her a moment later and then it was Gabriel's turn. His heart started pounding in his rib cage. His lungs could barely take in enough air, his chest was so tight. Once he stepped out of this plane, he was a coronation away from being *Su Majestad el Rey Don Gabriel I.* It was a terrifying prospect, but he pushed himself up out of his seat anyway.

Taking a deep breath, he stepped into the doorway. He was momentarily blinded by the sun. He paused for a moment to adjust, a smile on his face and his arm raised in greeting. He slowly made his way down the stairs, careful not to fall and make the worst possible impression. By the time he reached the bottom, he could look out into the crowd of photographers. There were about fifty of them gathered with cameras and video crews.

To the left and right of the stairs were two large gentlemen in military suits similar to the one Serafia had recently had tailored for him. In addition to their shiny brass buttons and collections of metals, they wore earpieces with cords that disappeared under their collars. He hadn't really given the idea of his personal security much thought until now.

The men bowed, and after he nodded to them both, they walked two paces behind Gabriel as he made his way down the carpet. At the end of the path, he could see his father and Serafia waiting for him with a man he presumed was his press secretary. Serafia had an exaggerated smile like a stage mom, reminding him to smile and wave.

He was almost to the end when a man with a video crew charged to the edge of the barricade and shouted to him. "Gabriel! How do you feel about your brother's abdication? Did you know he had a child on the way?"

The bold question startled him.

"Rafe made his choice. I don't blame him for

his decision." Serafia had told him he wasn't to answer questions, but he was thrown off guard with a film crew pointing the camera right in his face.

"What about the child?" the man pressed.

He felt a protectiveness build up inside him, his fists curling tight at his side. "I was unaware of the seriousness of his relationship with Ms. Fielding, but the matter of their child is their business, and I must insist that you respect their privacy."

"Have you chosen a queen yet?" Another reporter shouted before he could take another step. From there, it was a rapid fire he couldn't escape.

"Will she be a citizen of Alma or a member of a European royal family to strengthen trade agreements?"

"Did you leave a lover behind in America?"

Gabriel felt his throat close. He didn't know how to even begin addressing these questions, but he was certain his required smile had faded.

"Please!" Serafia shouted, stepping in front

of him and holding her hands up to the camera. "He's been in Del Sol for five minutes. Let's allow Don Gabriel to get settled in and perhaps coroneted before we start worrying about the line of succession, shall we?"

She took his arm and with a forceful tug, led him down the rug and inside the terminal. From there, security ushered them quickly out a side door to a black SUV with Alma's flag flying on each corner of the hood.

The door had barely shut before the convoy was on the road. The inside of the vehicle was quiet. He was stunned by the turn of events. Serafia was stiff beside him.

"What the hell was that?" his father finally asked.

"I didn't realize—" Gabriel began to defend himself to his father, but he realized he was looking at Serafia with eye daggers.

"You said there were to be no questions," Rafael snapped. "Why wasn't the press properly briefed?"

"They were," she argued, her spine lengthening in defiance. "Hector assured me that they were told Gabriel wasn't answering questions, but to tell them they can't ask is suppression of free press. No matter what they're told, reporters will ask questions in the hopes they can catch someone off guard and get an answer that will provide a juicy headline."

"Unacceptable."

Serafia sighed angrily. "I can assure you that I will work with Hector to have the offending reporters identified and will see to it that their press privileges are suspended."

"Gabriel should've been briefed. If you knew the press might push him for questions, he should've been better prepared. That's your job."

"I'm an image consultant, not his press secretary. What kind of briefing does he need to walk down a rug and wave? I suggest that when we arrive at the palace, we arrange to meet with Hector immediately. He'll need to be able to handle those sorts of things better in the future. There are more public appearances this week. We can't risk that happening again. I'm sorry that—"

"Stop," Gabriel said. He'd grown angrier with every apologetic word out of her mouth. There was no reason for her to ask for forgiveness. "You've done nothing wrong, Serafia. I apologize for my father's harsh, inappropriate tone. I should've anticipated they would ask questions like that. I will be more prepared next time. End of discussion. For now, let's just focus on getting settled in and prepared for our next event."

His father's sharp gaze raked over him as he spoke, the older man's tan Mediterranean complexion mottled with red. He was clearly angry his son had shut him down, but that was too bad. The balance of power had shifted in the family. The moment Gabriel stepped off that plane, he was in charge. They weren't in Miami anymore where his father ruled over the family with an iron fist.

They were in Alma now and Gabriel was going to be the king. His father had ruined his chance to be the boss when he divorced

Gabriel's mother without an annulment, so he'd better get used to the way things were going to be now. Gabriel was no longer the useless middle son who could be berated or ignored.

Gabriel was going to be king.

"It's beautiful," Serafia said as they entered the main room of the palace.

El Castillo del Arena was the official royal residence in Del Sol. Looking like a giant sandcastle, hence its name, it sat on a fortified wall overlooking the bay. The early Arabian influences on the architecture were evident everywhere you looked, from the arches to the intricate mosaic tile work. The inner courtyards had gardens that made a cool escape from the sun with lush trees, fountains and blooming flowers in every direction.

Clearly it wasn't as grand a palace as it had once been: the Persian rugs had threadbare corners and the upholstery on the furniture was worn and dirty. Seventy years in the hands of a dictatorship had made their mark, but it still had the grand design and details of its former glory. It wouldn't take long to restore the palace.

Few people had been allowed in under the Tantaberras. It was a pity. The grand rooms with the arched ceilings were begging for a royal event with all the elite of Alma in attendance.

From the expression on his face, Gabriel wasn't as impressed. Since the heated discussion in the car, he'd been quiet. She thought that when Señor Montoro skipped the tour and asked to be shown to his rooms so he could nap Gabriel would perk up, but he didn't. Now he silently took it all in as they followed his personal steward, Ernesto, on a tour through the palace.

"These are the king's private chambers," Ernesto said as he opened the double doors to reveal the expansive room.

There was a king-size bed in the center of the room with a massive four-poster frame. It was draped in red fabric with a dozen red and gold pillows scattered across the bed. Large tapestries hung on the walls, and a Moroccan rug covered the stone floors.

"Your bath and closet are through those doors," Ernesto continued.

She watched as Gabriel looked around, a slightly pained expression on his face. "It's awfully dark in here," he complained. "It's like a cave or an underground cellar. Are there only those two windows?"

Ernesto looked at the two arched windows crafted of stained glass and nodded. "Yes, Your Majesty."

She watched Gabriel tense at the use of the formal title. "I'm not king yet, Ernesto. You can just call me Gabriel."

The man's eyes grew wide. "I would rather not, Your Grace. You're still the crown prince."

"I suppose." Gabriel sighed and fixed his gaze on a set of double doors on the other side of the room. "Where do those doors go to?"

Ernesto, lean and dark-complexioned, moved quickly to the doors and opened them. "Through here are the queen's rooms. And beyond it are chambers for her ladies-in-waiting, although the rooms may be better suited in these times as an office or a nursery. The rooms haven't really been used since your great-grandmother, Queen Anna Maria, fled Alma."

Gabriel frowned. "The queen doesn't share a room with the king?"

"She may. Traditionally, having her own space allowed her to pursue more feminine activities with her ladies such as sewing or reading without interfering with the running of the state."

"It's like I've gone back in time," Gabriel grumbled, and ran his fingers through his hair in exasperation.

"The staff is still working on restoring and modernizing the palace. Perhaps Your Majesty would prefer to spend some time prior to the coronation at Playa del Onda. It's a more modern estate, built for the royal family to vacation at the beach in the summers. It's lovely, with floor-to-ceiling windows that overlook the sea and bright, open rooms."

For the first time since they'd arrived,

Serafia noticed Gabriel perk up. "How far is it from here?"

"It's about an hour's drive along the coastal highway, but you won't mind a minute of it. The views are exquisite. I can call ahead to the staff there and let them know you'll be coming if you'd like."

Gabriel considered his options for a moment and finally turned to look at Serafia. "I know we'll be coming back to Del Sol for a lot of activities this week, but I think I'd like to stay out there while I can. Care to continue our work at the beach?" he asked.

She nodded. The location wasn't important to her, but she could tell it mattered to him. He seemed to have a tense, almost claustrophobic reaction to his own quarters, despite the room being massive in scale with tall, arched ceilings. If he could relax, he would absorb more information. She could accommodate the extended drive times in their schedule.

"Then let's do that. My father will be staying here, but Señorita Espina and I will be going to

Playa del Onda. We'll be staying there for the next week. I'll return as we start preparing for the coronation."

"Very good. I'll arrange for your transportation."

"Ernesto?"

The steward paused. "Yes, Your Majesty?"

"See if you can arrange for a convertible with a GPS. I'd like to drive myself to the compound and enjoy the sun and sea air on the way."

"Drive yourself?" Ernesto seemed stumped for a moment, but then immediately shook off his concerns. It wasn't his place to question the king's requests. "Yes, Your Grace." He turned and disappeared down the hallway.

"They're not going to know what to do with a king like you," Serafia said.

"Me, neither," Gabriel noted dryly. "But maybe if we spend a couple days at the beach, we can all be better prepared for my official return to the palace."

They walked out of the king's chambers and down the winding staircase to the main hall.

Within minutes, they were greeted by the royal guard, who reported that they already had a car waiting for him outside. They would be following in the black SUV that brought him there.

Gabriel didn't argue. Instead they walked out into the courtyard. A cherry-red Peugeot convertible was parked there. "Whose car is this?" he asked as an attendant opened the door for Serafia to get in.

"It is Señor Ernesto's car, Your Majesty."

"What will he drive while I have it?"

"One of the royal fleet." The attendant pointed to an area with several vehicles parked there. "He is happy to let you borrow it. The address of the beach compound is already entered in the system, Your Majesty."

Gabriel took the keys, slipped out of his suit coat and got in beside her. He waited until the guard had assembled in the SUV behind them; then he started the car and they headed toward the gates.

Once they slipped beyond the fortress walls, Serafia noticed Gabriel's posture relax. It was as if a weight had been lifted from his shoulders. She couldn't help feeling the same way. Ernesto had been right: the view was amazing. Once they escaped Del Sol and started climbing up the mountain, everything changed. The winding coastal road showcased wide vistas with bright blue skies, turquoise waters and ships along the shoreline.

With the sun warming her skin and the ocean air whipping the strands of her hair around her face, she felt herself relax for the first time since she'd left Barcelona. Although the Atlantic islands were different from her Mediterranean hacienda, it felt as if she were back there, the place where she felt the most at home, and safe.

"Are you hungry?" he asked.

"Yes." They'd had croissants and juice on the plane, but it was past lunchtime now and she was starving.

Gabriel nodded. A mile up the road, he slowed and pulled off at a small, hole-in-the-wall restaurant overlooking the sea. A moment later, the royal guard pulled up beside them and lowered a window.

"Is there a problem, Your Majesty?" the one with the slicked-back brown hair who was driving the SUV asked.

"I'm hungry. Have you two had lunch?"

The two guards looked at each other in confusion and the driver turned back to him. "No, we haven't."

"Is this place any good?" he asked.

"I have eaten here many times, but in my opinion, it isn't fit for the king."

Gabriel looked at her and smiled widely. "Perfect. I'm starving. Let's all grab something to eat."

The two of them waited outside with the younger blond guard as the other went inside to make sure the restaurant was secure. It wasn't big enough to house much more than a tiny kitchen and a few tables on the veranda.

When they got the all-clear, a small, slow-moving old woman greeted them as they came in and gave them their choice of tables outside.

As Gabriel had insisted they eat as well, the guards took a table near the door to watch anyone coming in or out, allowing him and Serafia privacy while they dined.

The menu was limited, but the royal guard with the dark hair named Jorge recommended the *caldereta de langosta*. It was a seasonal lobster stew with tomatoes, onions, garlic and peppers, served with thin slices of bread.

They all ordered the caldereta and Serafia was not disappointed. Normally she gave great care and thought into every bite she put in her mouth, but the stew was too amazing to worry about it. The lobster was soft and buttery in texture, while spicy in flavor thanks to the peppers. The bread soaked up the broth perfectly and helped carry the large pieces of lobster to her mouth without her wearing most of it on her pale taupe suit.

"This is wonderful," she said, when she was more than halfway finished with her stew. "Thank you for stopping."

"I was getting cranky," Gabriel said. He

glanced over the railing at the sparking blue sea below them. "If I can be cranky looking at a view like this, I've got to be hungry."

"I would've thought the incident this morning had more to do with it than hunger."

"This morning was nothing and my father wanted to make it into something. I have enough to worry about without him making you uncomfortable. You've gone out of your way to help me through this. You've tolerated my bad moods and my childish behavior. I think I will be a better king for what you've done, so I should be thanking you, not criticizing you."

Serafia was stunned by his thoughtful words. He seemed to be almost a different person since they'd arrived in Alma. Or at least since the moment he'd stood up to his father. He had seemed to grow taller in that moment, physically stronger even, as he sat in the vehicle. Perhaps he truly was gaining the confidence he needed to rule Alma.

"Thank you," she said. "I appreciate that. And I appreciate you standing up for me this morning. The look on your father's face when you put an end to the discussion was priceless, really."

Gabriel looked at her with a wry grin. "It was good, wasn't it? It's the first time I've stood up to him in my whole life and I'm glad I did."

"Is he always like that?"

Gabriel sipped his sparkling water and nodded. "Nothing was ever good enough for my father, but especially me. I could never understand it growing up. I did everything right, everything he wanted me to do. I went to school where he wanted me to go, took the position at the company he wanted me to have. I let him banish me to South American Operations. After everything that happened there, I almost got the feeling he was disappointed I came back. I've never understood why."

"After everything that happened there?" Gabriel seemed to be alluding to some incident she was unaware of. "What happened?"

With a sigh, he popped the last of his bread in his mouth and shook his head. "It doesn't matter. What matters is that I learned some valuable lessons. First, that you have to be careful who you can trust. And second, that I'm a grown man who can live and do however I please. These last few years my behavior has just been written off by my family as reckless and selfish, but it's been good for me. If my father doesn't approve of me either way, I should do whatever I want to, right?"

Serafia suppressed her frown. How had she not seen how wounded he was before now? The cracks in his facade were starting to show and they made her wonder what had turned the obedient middle son into the rebellious, distant one. He didn't want to talk about it and she understood. She had dark secrets of her own, but she couldn't help wondering if his past and its effect on him might hinder his leadership in Alma.

"I never wanted to be king, but now that I'm here, I think this might work out. My father may still disagree with what I do and how, but now I don't have to listen to it any longer." Abruptly standing, he pulled some euros from his wallet and threw them down on the table to cover everyone's lunch tab. Serafia got up as well, placing her napkin on the table.

"Let's get back on the road."

Five

"You look very handsome tonight."

Serafia stood at Gabriel's side and looked over the railing at the crowd below. There was a sea of people there, all dressed in their finest tuxedos and gowns. A string quartet was in the corner, filling the large space with a soothing background melody. It was a glittering display of marble floors, towering flower arrangements and twinkling crystal chandeliers. Patrick Rowling spared no expense when it came to his home or the parties he hosted there.

They had arrived at the Rowling mansion via a side door and were escorted upstairs to wait in

Patrick's library so Gabriel could make a grand entrance. To their right was an elaborate marble staircase that twisted its way into the center of the ballroom. It just begged for a king to stroll down with a regal air.

Regal was not the vibe she was getting from Gabriel. Her compliment seemed to unnerve him. He shifted uncomfortably under her scrutiny, although there was no reason for him to be nervous. The ceremonial dress had been tailored beautifully and despite his complaints, he looked noble, powerful and very appropriate for a party like this. He had come a long way in the last week and she'd felt a swell of pride in her chest when he stepped out of his bedroom in full regalia earlier.

"I still feel like Prince Charming at the ball. And from the look of the crowd here tonight, all the eligible young maidens have come to land a king for a husband."

"I did notice that," she admitted. There were a lot of young women at the party, all painted and coiffed to the max. Decked out in an array of eye-catching jewel-tone silks and satins, they were like parading peacocks among the dark tuxedos. If Serafia had to guess, she'd say that millions of dollars had been laid out tonight in the hopes that they might catch the future king's eye.

She had gone the opposite route. Her gown was a very soft pink, almost a blush color. The organza ruching wrapped around her body, dotted with tiny crystals and beads. While sedate in color, it still had a few scandalous details like a plunging V-cut neckline and a slit on the side that almost reached the top of her thigh. She wanted to look as if she belonged, but she didn't want to stand out. She wasn't here to enjoy a party; she was here to help Gabriel get through his first real event in Alma.

"It certainly looks like you have your pick of ladies here tonight."

"Do I?"

Serafia turned to look at him and was surprised to see the serious way he was looking at her. He had the same heated intensity in his eyes he'd had the day he pinned her against the armoire. What exactly did he mean by that? She couldn't possibly be his pick when there were so many younger, more attractive women in the room tonight. "I…uh…" She hesitated. "I… think you've got a lot to choose from and a long night ahead of you. Don't make a decision too quickly. Keep your options open."

Gabriel sighed and turned away to look at the crowd. "I'll try."

A man in a tuxedo approached them on the landing and bowed to Gabriel. "If Your Majesty is ready, I'll cue the musicians to announce your arrival."

"Yes, I suppose it's time."

"May I escort you downstairs, Señorita Espina?"

"Yes, thank you." She took the man's arm and turned back to Gabriel. "I'll see you downstairs after the guests have all been presented."

"You're not going down with me?"

Serafia chuckled. "This is like the arrival at the airport, but without the pushy reporters.

You need to have your moment. Alone." She wouldn't make many new girlfriends tonight if she showed up on the king's arm and beat them all to the punch.

"Good luck," she said, giving him a wink before carefully descending the staircase and joining the crowd. She parted with her escort, finding a spot at the edge of the room near one of the royal guards to watch Gabriel's entrance.

The orchestra started playing Alma's national anthem. The bustling crowd immediately grew silent and everyone turned their gaze to the flag hanging from the second-floor railing. When the last note died out, Gabriel appeared at the top of the stairs looking as much like a king as a man raised to have the position.

"His Royal Highness, El Príncipe Gabriel, the future El Rey Don Gabriel the First of Alma."

The crowd applauded as he came down the stairs. The air in the room was electric with excitement. Gabriel didn't fully appreciate how important this was for the people of Alma. They were free, and his arrival was the living, breathing evidence of that freedom. People bowed and curtseyed as he passed.

"Oh my God, he's so handsome. I didn't think it was possible, but he's even more attractive than Rafe."

Serafia turned to see a young woman and her mother standing nearby. The woman was maybe twenty-three and she was in a sapphire-blue gown that looked amazing with her golden skin and flaxen hair. Her mother was an older carbon copy in a more sedate silver gown. They were both dripping with diamonds, but the twinkle in their eyes sparkled even brighter as they looked at Gabriel.

"Oh, Dita," the mother gushed. "He's perfect for you. This is your big chance tonight. You look absolutely flawless, better than any of the other girls here." She looked around the room, scanning the competition again. Her gaze lit on Serafia for only a moment, then moved on as though she were an insignificant presence. Apparently the woman didn't read *Vogue*, or she would realize she was standing beside a former supermodel.

Serafia recognized *her*, however. At the mention of her daughter's name, she realized the mother was Felicia Gomez. The Gomez family was one of the richest in Alma, although unlike the Rowlings, they were natives like the Espinas. Many of the wealthier families had fled Alma when Tantaberra came to power, but the Gomez family had stayed.

Serafia had never met them, but she had heard her mother talk about them from time to time. It was rarely flattering. She got the impression that they were fair-weather friend types who worked hard to ingratiate themselves with whoever was in power. She didn't know what they had to do to maintain their money and lands under the dictatorship, but she was certain it was a price the Espinas wouldn't have paid.

It would not surprise her mother at all to know they were here on the hunt for a rich husband. With the dictatorship dissolved, they had to put themselves in a good position with the new royal family, and what better way than to marry into it? Serafia took a step closer to listen in as Felicia continued her instructions to Dita.

"When we're introduced to the king, remember everything I've told you. You've got to make a good impression on him. Be coquettish, but not too aggressive. Make eye contact, but don't hold it for too long. Make him come to you and then you'll have him like putty in your hands. It worked on your father. It will work on him. You deserve to be queen, always remember that."

Serafia tried not to chuckle. She was certain a similar conversation was taking place all over the room. There were easily thirty bright-eyed girls here with their parents. All were after the same prize. Serafia might be the only single woman in the room who wasn't on the hunt. She had no interest in competing with a bunch of little girls for Gabriel's attention.

When Gabriel reached the bottom of the stairs, he was greeted by his father and Patrick Rowling. They escorted him over to a raised dais on the far side of the room. They took their seats there and the crowd gathered for a receiving line. Everyone was excited for their chance to be introduced to the new king.

Serafia took advantage of the distraction to go to the empty bar. She got glasses of wine for them both, hugging the edge of the room to deliver the drink to Gabriel. As she got close, Patrick was introducing his sons, William and James, to Gabriel and his father. Will was Patrick's heir apparent to the oil and real estate empire they'd built. James, like Gabriel, was the second son, the spare heir, even though he was born only minutes after his twin brother.

Neither of the men looked particularly happy to be here tonight. Even then, they seemed more comfortable than Gabriel. He kept cycling between a stiff regal pose, a slightly slumped-over bored stance and a fidgety anxious carriage that made it obvious to Serafia that he was very uncomfortable. Perhaps a glass of wine would be enough to relax him without loosening his tongue too much.

Out of the corner of her eye, Serafia spied

one of the party's many servers. The petite girl with chin-length black hair was lurking along the edge of the room, her gaze focused fully on the Rowling brothers as they greeted the king.

It took a moment, but Serafia was finally able to wave her over. As a model, she was used to towering over people, but the server was probably close to five feet tall, a little pixie of a thing with sparkling dark eyes that immediately caught Serafia's attention. On her immaculately pressed black shirt, she wore a small brass nametag that read *Catalina*.

"Yes, ma'am?"

"Would you please take this wine to Prince Gabriel?" Serafia placed the wine on her tray.

Catalina took a deep breath and nodded. "Of course," she said, immediately departing. Well trained, she waited until Will and James were escorted away, slipping over quietly to deliver the drink, then disappearing so quickly that some people might not have even seen her.

Gabriel took a heavy sip of the wine, searching Serafia out in the crowd. When his gaze lit on her, Serafia felt a chill run down her spine. Goose bumps rose across her bare arms, making her rub them self-consciously. He winked at her, and before she could prompt him to smile, he broke out his practiced grin and turned to the next family being presented.

Serafia had to admit she was pleased with the results of her work. In only a week, they had managed to smooth over his rough edges and mold him into a man fit to be royalty. As she watched him interact with the Gomez family and the young and beautiful Dita, she couldn't help the pang of jealousy inside her.

Perhaps she had done too good a job. She had polished away all the reasons she needed to stay far, far away from Gabriel Montoro.

Gabriel was exhausted. All he'd done for the last hour was get introduced to people, but he was done. He was tired of smiling, tired of greeting people. It wasn't as if he was going to be able to remember a single name once each person turned away and the next was presented.

Unfortunately there were hours left in the night. Now started the dancing and the mingling. With the formalities out of the way, people would seek him out for more casual discussions. The ladies would expect him to solicit a dance or two.

He did none of those things. Instead he sought out another glass a wine and a few bites from the buffet of canapés and fresh fruits. He was hoping to find Serafia, who had disappeared at some point, but instead his father cornered him at the baked brie.

"What do you think of William?"

William? Gabriel went through the two hundred names he'd just heard and drew a blank.

"William Rowling, Patrick's oldest son," Rafael clarified, seemingly irritated with Gabriel for dismissing the Rowlings so easily.

"Oh," Gabriel said, taking a sip of wine. He refrained from mentioning to his father that he couldn't tell the two brothers apart. That would just agitate him. "He seemed very nice. Why?

Are you trying to fix me up with him? He's really not my type, Dad."

"Gabriel," Rafael said in a warning tone. "I was thinking about him and Bella."

Gabriel tried not to frown at his father. All this royalty nonsense was going to his father's head if he thought he could start arranging marriages and no one would question it. "I think Bella would have a great deal more to say on the subject than I would."

"Rowling is the most powerful businessman in Alma. Combining our families would strengthen our position here, both financially and socially. If he had a daughter I'd be shoving her under your nose, too."

"Dad, it's a marriage, not a business merger."

"Same difference. I had a similar arrangement with your mother and now our company is in the Fortune 500."

"*And* you're divorced," Gabriel added. Their mother was living happily on another continent and had been since Bella turned eighteen and she had fulfilled her obligation to Rafael and the children. That was just what Bella would want for her own marriage, Gabriel was sure. Turning from his father, he scanned the crowd again.

"Who are you looking for?" Rafael pressed.

"Serafia."

Rafael popped a shrimp into his mouth and chewed it with a sour expression. "Don't get too dependent on her, Gabriel. She's just here through the end of the week. You've got to learn to stand on your own without her."

Gabriel was taken aback by his father's words. What did he care as long as Gabriel parroted all the right words and did all the right things? "I'm not dependent on her. I simply enjoy her company and I'm finding this party tedious without her."

"Yes, well, don't get too involved on that front, either. If you're bored, I suggest you focus on the ladies here tonight. Take Dita Gomez or Mariella Sanchez for a spin around the dance floor and see if you feel differently."

"And what if I want to take Serafia for a spin around the dance floor, Father? Stop treating her like she's just an employee. The Espinas are just as important a noble family in Alma as any of these others."

His father stiffened and the red blotchiness Gabriel had seen so often lately started climbing up his neck. "Now is not the time to discuss things like this," he hissed in a low voice. "Now is the time to mingle with your new countrymen and start your search for a suitable queen. We will talk about the Espina family later. Now go mingle!" he demanded.

Gabriel didn't bother arguing with him. If mingling meant he could get away from his father for a while, he'd do it gladly. Perhaps he'd find where Serafia was hiding in the process. With a nod, he set aside his plate and ventured out into the crowd. Every few feet he was stopped by someone and engaged in polite banter. How did he like Alma so far? Did the weather suit him? Had he had the opportunity to enjoy the beaches or any of the local culture?

He was halfway through one of these discussions when he spied Serafia over the man's shoulder. She was standing across the room chatting with a gentleman whose name he had immediately forgotten when they were introduced in the receiving line.

Gabriel had seen a lot of beautiful women tonight, but he just couldn't understand how his father could think that any of them could hold a candle to Serafia. She was breathtaking, catwalk perfection. Sure, she wasn't as rail-thin as she had been in her modeling days, but the pounds had just softened the angles and filled out the curves that her gown clung to. The pale pink of her dress was like soft rose petals scattered across her olive complexion. It was a delicate, romantic color, unlike all the bold look-at-me dresses the other women were wearing.

Serafia didn't need that for men to look at her, at least for Gabriel to look at her. He had a hard time looking anywhere else. Her silky black hair was loose tonight in shiny curls that fell over her shoulders and down her back. She wore very little jewelry—just a pair of pink sapphire studs at her ears—but between the beads of her dress and the glitter of her delicate pink lipstick, she seemed to sparkle from head to toe.

He felt his mouth go dry as he imagined her leaving a trail of glittering pink lipstick down his bare stomach. He wanted to pull her body hard against his and bury his fingers in the inky black silk of her hair. For all he cared, this party and these people could disappear. He wanted to be alone with Serafia and not for etiquette lessons or strategy discussions.

He hadn't given much thought to the man she was speaking to, but when he laid a hand on Serafia's upper arm, Gabriel felt his blood pressure spike with jealousy. Quickly excusing himself from the conversation he'd been ignoring, he moved through the room, arriving at her side in an instant.

Serafia's eyes widened at his sudden arrival. She took a step back, introducing him to the man she was speaking to. "Your Majesty, may I reintroduce you to Tomás Padillo? He owns Padillo Vineyards, where we'll be taking a tour tomorrow afternoon. I was just telling him how much you've enjoyed the Manto Negro from his winery since you arrived."

"Ah yes," Gabriel replied with a nod of recognition. He held up his glass. "Is this a vintage of yours, as well?"

"Yes, Your Majesty, that's my award-winning Chardonnay. I'm honored to have you drink it and looking forward to hosting your visit with us tomorrow."

The man seemed harmless enough; then again, Gabriel didn't see a ring on the man's hand. He didn't intend to leave Serafia alone with him.

"I'm looking forward to it, as well. May I steal away Miss Espina?" he asked.

"Of course, Your Majesty."

Gabriel nodded and scooped up Serafia's arm into his own. He led her away into a quiet corner behind the staircase where they could talk.

"Is everything going all right?" she asked.

Gabriel nodded. "I think so. My dad is pressuring me to mingle with the ladies, but I haven't gotten that far yet."

Serafia sighed and patted his forearm. "You've done your fair share of wooing ladies, Gabriel. This shouldn't be very difficult for you."

"That was different," he argued. "Picking up a woman at a nightclub for a little fun is nothing like shopping for a wife. It feels more like a hunt anyway, except I'm the fox. I'm surprised one of the hounds hasn't ferretted me out from our hiding place by now. Would you stay with me for a while?"

"Not while you dance!"

"Of course not. But go around with me while I mingle for a while. I think I'll be more comfortable that way. You might remember people's names."

"Gabriel, you need to be able to—"

"Please…" he said, looking into her eyes with his most pathetic expression.

"Okay, but you have to promise me you will ask no fewer than two ladies to dance tonight. No moms or grandmothers, either. Eligible, single women of marrying age. And not me, either," she seemed to add for good measure.

"If I dance with two women who meet your criteria, would you be willing to dance with me just for fun?"

Serafia gave him a stern look, but the smile that teased at the corners of her full lips gave her away. "Maybe. But you've got to put in a good effort out there. You're looking for a queen, remember. If you don't find a good one, your father will do it for you, like poor Bella."

"You've heard about that?" Gabriel asked.

"Yes. I overheard Patrick discussing the idea of it with Will."

"How'd he take it?"

"About as well as Bella would, I expect. But my point is that you need to get out there and make that decision yourself."

"Fair enough." Offering her his arm, he led them back into the main area of the room. As they slipped through the crowd, he leaned down to whisper in her ear, "Who would you choose for me? Where should I start?"

Serafia looked thoughtfully around the room, her gaze falling on a buxom, almost chubby redhead whose fiery hair was in direct contrast to her personality. She was a shy wallflower of a girl who had barely met his gaze when they were introduced.

"Start with Helena Ruiz. Her family is in the seafood business and they provide almost all the fresh fish and shellfish to the area and to parts of Spain and Portugal, as well. And," she added, "unlike the others, she seems to be *reluctantly* hunting for a husband. She reminds me very much of a lot of the girls I work with in my business. Choosing her first might be good for her social standing and her self-esteem."

Gabriel was pleased with Serafia's choice and her reasoning behind it. It was one of the things about her that really stuck with him. She wasn't just concerned about making over his outside, but his inside, as well. In their training sessions, they'd discussed charities he'd like to support and causes he wanted to rally behind as king. Parliament and the prime minister would draft and enforce the laws of Alma, but as king, he would have a major influence over the hearts and minds of the people. He had a platform, so he needed to be prepared to have a cause.

In such a short time, Serafia had not just made over his wardrobe. She had made over his soul. He felt like a better person, a person more deserving of a woman like her. He'd never felt that way before in his entire life. He'd always been second to Rafe, not good enough in his father's eyes. His mother had recognized the value in him, but even she couldn't sway his father's opinion.

Since he returned home from Venezuela after the kidnapping, he'd been a different man. He'd stopped seeking everyone's approval, especially his father's. With his mother traveling the world and unable to call him on it, he'd settled happily into his devil-may-care lifestyle. It had suited him well and no one had questioned the change in him. But Serafia had. She had the ability to see through all his crap, and it made him think that perhaps he could open up to her, really trust her, unlike so many others in his life.

As he left her side and approached the doe-eyed Helena, he knew Serafia had made the right choice. The bright, genuine smile on the girl's face and the pinched, jealous expressions of some of the other girls proved that much. He led her out onto the dance floor for the first official dance of the evening. Helena was nearly trembling in his arms, but he reassured her with a smile and a wink.

Serafia made him want to be a better man. She helped him become a better man. He could think of no other woman who should be at his side but her. And he would tell her that.

Tonight.

Six

"Okay," a voice announced over Serafia's shoulder. "I have met your requirements."

She turned to find Gabriel standing behind her. She'd been expecting his arrival. It had been nearly two hours since she sent him out onto the dance floor with Helena Ruiz. He had danced with her and at least five other ladies Serafina had chosen for him. Her inner spiteful streak had led her not to choose Dita as one of the dance partners. She wasn't entirely sure if it was because she knew the Gomezes were disingenuous, or if it was because the idea of him dancing and potentially falling for the statuesque beauty made her blood boil.

"You have," she said with a pleased smile. "You've more than met them. You've exceeded them. Well done, Your Majesty. Any pique your interest?"

Gabriel arched an eyebrow at her and held out his hand. "Join me on the dance floor and I'll tell you."

There were quite a few pairs dancing now, so the two of them would not stand out as much as they would have earlier. Deciding there was no harm in it—and she had promised—she took his hand and followed him out into the center of the dance floor.

Gabriel slipped his arm around her waist and cupped her hand with his own. For the first twenty seconds or so of the dance, she found she could hardly breathe. Her bare skin sizzled where they touched, and her heart was racing in her chest. Fortunately Gabriel was a strong lead and she didn't have to think too much about her feet. She simply followed him across the floor and focused internally on suppressing the physical reaction she had to his touch.

"So, find any chemistry out on the dance floor?" she asked, desperate for a distraction.

"Not until now," he said, his green gaze burrowing into her own.

"Gabriel," she scolded, but he shook his head as though he wasn't having any of that.

"Don't start. I've had enough of the reasons why I can't have what I want. I don't really care. All I know is that I want you."

The power of his words struck her like a wave and she struggled to argue against it. "No, you don't."

"Are you honestly going to stand there and tell me you know my feelings better than I do?"

She shook her head, focusing her gaze on the golden ropes at his shoulder instead of the intensity in his eyes. "You might want me for tonight, for one of your one-night flings, but not for your queen."

"Do we have to decide what it will be tonight?"

If she had to decide in the moment, she would say no. She was wrapped up in the sensation of being so close to him. Her body was rebelling against her, desiring him desperately even as she argued against the very idea of it. "You aren't in Miami anymore, Gabriel. Every eye in the room is on you tonight. This feeling for me will pass and then you can focus on making a smart decision about your future. A future without me."

"Serafia, you are beautiful. You're the most stunning woman I've ever seen in real life or on a magazine cover. You're graceful, elegant, thoughtful, smart and incredibly insightful. I don't know why you find it so hard to believe that I could want you so desperately."

Desperately? Her gaze met his, her lips parting softly in surprise. His words were said with such sincerity, but she simply didn't believe a single one. She was too aware of her own faults to do that. She'd spent too many years having every aspect of her appearance ripped apart by modeling experts, their voices far louder than any of her fans' praises. And even if he could see past all her imperfections, he didn't know how broken she was. The truth of her past would send any man running. "You don't want me, Gabriel. You want your teenage fantasy from ten years ago. That person doesn't exist anymore."

She pulled away from his grasp as the music ended and made her way through the crowd of people coming on and off the dance floor. Spying a set of French doors, she opened them and slipped outside into the large courtyard of the Rowling mansion. She kept going, following a path into the gardens. It was landscaped like the formal English gardens of Patrick's homeland, so she continued on a gravel path along a long line of neatly trimmed shrubs until she came upon a clearing and a circular fountain.

She collapsed onto the stone ledge of the fountain and took a deep breath. She felt much calmer out here, away from the crush of people in the ballroom, but the sense of relief didn't last long. Not a minute later, she heard the sound of footsteps on the gravel and spied Gabriel coming toward her on the garden path.

He approached silently and sat on the edge of the fountain beside her. She expected him to immediately give her the third degree for running out on him. It was incredibly rude, after all, and she kept forgetting he was the king. People were probably inside talking about her hasty departure.

But Gabriel didn't seem to be in a hurry. He seemed to enjoy the garden as well, taking a deep breath and gazing up at the blanket of stars overhead. She did the same, relaxing as she tried to identify different constellations. Looking at the stars always made her problems seem less important, less significant. The universe was a big place.

When he finally got around to speaking, Serafia was ready to answer his questions. She was tired of hiding her illness, anyway. She might as well put it all out there, warts and all. It would likely put an end to their pointless flirtation and she could stop torturing herself with possibilities that didn't really exist.

"What was that all about in there? Really? Why is it so impossible that I would want you as you are, right now?"

"It's impossible for me to believe it because I know how seriously messed up I am, Gabriel. The truth is that I don't have a congenital heart defect and I didn't spend a year having surgeries to correct it."

Gabriel frowned at her. "Well, then, what really happened to you?"

Serafia sighed and shook her head. "No one knows the truth but my family and my doctors. My parents thought it would be easier for me if we told everyone the cover story, but that was all a lie. I had a heart attack on that runway because I had slowly and systematically tried to kill myself to be beautiful. The modeling industry is so high pressure and I couldn't stand up to it. I swallowed the lies they told me along with the prescription diet pills. I barely ate. I exercised six to eight hours a day. I abused cocaine, laxatives…anything that I thought would give me an edge and help me drop those last few pounds. My quest to be thinner, to be prettier, almost made me a very attractive corpse."

She was terrified to say the words aloud, but at the same time, it felt as if a weight was lifted from her chest. "The day I collapsed on the runway, I was five foot nine and ninety-three pounds. I was nothing but a walking skeleton and I received more compliments that morning than I ever had before. After I collapsed, I knew I had to leave the modeling industry because the environment was just too toxic. I had to spend a year in rehab and inpatient therapy for anorexia. I had to be completely reprogrammed, like I'd left some kind of cult."

Gabriel didn't recoil or react to her words. He just listened until she got it all out. "Are you better now?" he asked.

That was a difficult question to answer. Like an alcoholic, the danger of falling off the wagon was always there. "I've learned to manage. I've put so much strain on my heart that my day-to-day life is a very delicate balancing act. But for the most part, yes, the worst of it is behind me."

He sat studying her face for a few minutes. "I can't believe anyone had the audacity to tell you that you were anything but flawless. I mean, you're *Serafia*—supermodel extraordinaire, catwalk goddess and record holder for most *Vogue Italia* covers."

Once again, she started to squirm under his praise. "When you say things like that, Gabriel, it's really difficult for me to listen and even harder for me to accept. I was told for so long that I was fat and ugly and would never make it in the business. Even when I made it to the top, there's always someone there to try and knock you down. The modeling industry can be so venomous. You're never thin enough, pretty enough, talented enough, and both your competition and your customers feed you those criticisms every day. You believe something after you hear it enough times. Even all these years later, after all the therapy, there's a part of me that still believes that and thinks everything you're saying is just insincere flattery."

Gabriel reached out and covered her hand with his own. It was comforting and she was thankful for it, even as it surprised her. She expected him to finally see her flaws and run, but he didn't.

"It might be flattery, Serafia, but it's true. Every word. If I have to say it each day until you finally believe it, I will. I know how hard it can be to trust someone once that faith is abused. Once it's lost, it's almost impossible to get back, but I want to help you try."

There was a pain in his expression as he spoke. The lines deepened in his forehead with his frown. She knew something had happened to him in South America. Perhaps now, perhaps here, after she'd told her story, he might finally tell her his. "How do you know? What happened to you, Gabriel?"

With a sigh, he sat back and looked up at the sliver of a moon overhead. "I was fresh from college and my father named me VP of South

American Operations. As part of my job, I had to travel to our various shipping and trade ports in Brazil, Argentina, Venezuela and Chile. Dealing with Venezuela was controversial, but my father had decided that the country had oil and needed it shipped. Why shouldn't we profit from it instead of someone else?

"I saved Caracas for my last stop and things had gone so well in the other locations that I wasn't wary any longer by the time I arrived in Venezuela. I went down there and spent a few days getting acclimated and met with the team there. One evening, my guide and translator, Raoul, offered to take me out for an authentic Venezuelan dinner. The moment we stepped outside, a van pulled up by the curb. Raoul hit me on the back of the head with something and I blacked out. The next thing I knew, I was lying on a stinky, lumpy mattress in a cold, dark room with no windows. My wrists and ankles were tied with thick rope."

Serafia could barely believe what she was being told. How had she never heard about this before? She wanted to ask, but she didn't dare interrupt.

"When my captor finally showed up a few hours later, he told me that I was being held for ransom and as soon as my family paid them, I'd be released."

"Did they pay them?" she asked.

He avoided her gaze, swallowing hard before he spoke. "No. I was in that underground room in virtual darkness for over a week. Every day the guy would come down and bring me a jug of water and some food, but that was it. After about the sixth day alone with my thoughts, and with constant taunts from my captor that my family hadn't paid the ransom yet and must not care if I lived or died, I came to the conclusion that if I wanted out of this place, I'd have to save myself. And I decided that when I did, I was going to live the life I wanted from that moment on."

"You escaped?" Serafia asked, near breathless with suspense.

"My rusty metal bed frame was my savior.

I used it to slowly cut through my bindings. It took almost all day to do it. When my captor opened the door to bring my evening meal, I was waiting for him. I leaped on him, beating his head against the concrete floor until he stopped fighting me. Once I was sure he was unconscious, I took his gun and keys, locking him in the room. It turned out he was my only guard, so I literally went up the stairs and walked out onto the busy streets of Caracas. I made my way to the US embassy, told them what had happened and I was back in Miami by sunrise."

Serafia was nearly speechless. "Did they ever catch the people responsible?"

"Raoul was arrested for his part in the conspiracy, but he was just a facilitator paid a flat fee for delivering me at a special place and time. They found my captor still locked in the room where they kept me. Anyone else who was involved got away with it. But really, in the end, I wasn't angry with them. I was angry with my family. They knew what could happen if they sent me down there."

"What did they say when you showed up at home?"

Gabriel stiffened beside her and shrugged. "They welcomed me home and then tried to pretend it never happened. But I could never forget."

It was a horrible story to hear, but suddenly so much of Gabriel's personality suddenly made sense to her. He never got close to anyone and got a lot of grief from his family for being superficial. Even Serafia had been guilty of judging him, thinking he cared more about partying than worrying about anything serious. She'd accused him of being reckless, but when they were both faced with death, they reacted differently. She became supercautious, nearly afraid to live life for fear of losing it for good. He had done the opposite: living every moment to the fullest in case it was his last. Who was she to judge him?

Serafia reached out and took his hand. She felt

a surge of emotion when they touched. When she looked at him, for the first time she was able to see the sadness in his green eyes, the wariness behind the bright smile. The bad boy facade kept people away and she had fallen for it. She didn't want to keep him at arm's length any longer.

Gabriel gripped her hand in his, letting his thumb brush across her skin. It sent a shiver of awareness down her spine, urging her to lean in closer to him.

"I know that's a lot of information to process," he said. "I didn't tell it to you so you'd feel bad for me. I told you because I wanted you to understand that we're coming from a similar place. No one is perfect. We're all messed up somehow. But it's how we deal with it that matters. I'm an expert at pushing people away. You're the first woman I've ever met who had made me want to try to trust someone again. Stop thinking that you don't measure up somehow, because you're wrong."

Serafia gasped at his bold words. She couldn't

hold back any longer. She lunged forward, pressing her lips against his own before she lost her nerve. It had been a long time since she had trusted herself in all the various areas of her life, and romance had fallen to the bottom of the stack. What good was she to a man in the state she was in? Especially a prince? Still, she couldn't help herself. And neither could Gabriel.

He met her kiss with equal enthusiasm. He held her face in his hands, drawing her closer and drinking her in. He groaned against her lips and then let his tongue slip along hers. His touch made her insides turn molten with need and wore away the last of her self-control.

At last, Gabriel pulled away, their rapid breaths hovering between them in the night air. "Is it too early to make our exit?" he asked.

Serafia shook her head and looked into his eyes. "I think the prince can leave whenever he wants to."

It wasn't as simple to leave as Gabriel had hoped. He'd had to make the rounds, thank

Patrick for his hospitality and avoid the cutting glares of his father, but within half an hour, he and Serafia were in the back of the royal limousine on their way home to Playa del Onda.

When they climbed inside, Gabriel couldn't look away from the high slit in her pink gown and how it climbed nearly to her hip as she sat. He wanted to run his hands over that bare skin. His palms tingled with the need to reach for her, but there was a forty-five-minute drive home from the Rowling Estate.

Eyeballing the limousine's tinted partition, Gabriel called out to his driver, "We're going to need a little privacy back here, please."

"Of course, Your Majesty." In an instant, the heavily tinted glass slid up, blocking them from their driver's view and making for a more private drive home.

"What are you doing?" Serafia asked.

Gabriel turned to her, placing his hand on her knee. "I want you. Right now. I can't wait until we get back."

"We're in a car, Gabriel. The driver is right

there. The royal guard are in the SUV right behind us."

"They can't see us." His hand glided higher up her leg, brushing at the sensitive skin of her inner thigh. "Whether or not the driver *hears* us is up to you."

"I don't know about this," Serafia said, biting her full bottom lip.

Gabriel brushed his fingertips along the lacy barrier of her panties, making her gasp. "You may have reformed me, but there's still a little bad boy inside me." He stroked harder, making her stiffen and close her eyes. He leaned into her, placing a searing kiss against her neck before he whispered, "Let's both be bad tonight."

He gripped one strap of her gown, easing it down her shoulder, and then dipped his head to taste her flesh, nibbling on the column of her throat, the hollow behind her ear and the round of her shoulder. He slipped one hand behind her, finding the zipper of her gown and tugging it down enough to allow her gown to slip farther and expose the round globes of her large breasts.

They were more glorious than he'd ever imagined after seeing her in bikinis and skimpy gowns on magazine covers. "So beautiful," he murmured as his gaze devoured her. They were full and heavy, tipped with tight mocha nipples that he immediately covered with his hands and then his mouth.

Serafia bit her lip hard to keep from crying out as his tongue flicked across her skin. He teased her flesh, and then sucked hard at her breast. The hand he'd kept beneath her gown continued to stroke her, finally slipping under the lacy edge of her panties to feel the moist heat of her desire hiding beneath it.

"Gabriel!" she exclaimed in a hoarse whisper.

"Just lie back and enjoy it," he replied, turning with her as she leaned back across the seat to rest on her elbows. When she shifted her hips, he was better able to slide her gown out of the way and part her thighs. He stopped touching her only long enough to slip off her panties.

When he returned, he leaned down, parted her flesh and stroked her with his tongue. Serafia squirmed and writhed against him, but he didn't let up. He wrapped his arms around her thighs to hold her steady as he teased at her sensitive flesh again and again. Gabriel waited until he had her hovering on the edge; then he slipped one finger inside her. It sent her tumbling over, gasping and whimpering as quietly as she could manage while her release rocked through her.

When at last her body stilled except for her rapid breaths, Gabriel pulled away. While she recovered, he unbuttoned his suit pants and tugged them down. Reaching into his back pocket, he pulled a condom from his wallet and slipped it over the length of him. When he turned back to Serafia, she was watching him with a twinkle of deviousness in her dark eyes.

He reached for her and tugged her into his lap, her thighs straddling him as the limousine raced down the highway. Gabriel gripped her waist as she eased down and pushed him inside her. He gritted his teeth and pressed desperate fingertips into her flesh as he fought for control. She felt amazing. When he was buried fully inside her, he held her still for a moment, then reached for her face. He pulled her forward and captured her lips with his own.

As his tongue slipped inside her mouth and stroked her, he started moving slowly beneath her. Pushing the pink organza of her gown out of the way, he gripped the curve of her rear to guide her hips. At first, their movements were deliciously slow, and he savored every pang of pleasure. As the intensity built, they moved more frantically. Serafia grasped his shoulders and threw her head back, a silent cry in her throat.

"Let go for me," Gabriel pressed. "I want to watch it happen. You're so beautiful when you come undone."

She found her release again. This time, he held her close, not just watching, but feeling the pleasurable tremors running through her body and experiencing them with her. Her inner muscles tightened around him, coaxing his own release. As she collapsed against him, he wrapped his arms around her waist and thrust into her one last time. He buried his face in her neck, growling his climax against her flushed skin.

They sat together, not moving for several minutes. In the stillness, Gabriel was finally able to mentally catch up with everything that had happened in the last few hours.

The moment he had stepped out into the garden after her, he knew things would be different. He wasn't going to let her keep pulling away from him, and if opening up to her about his own past was what it took, he was willing to do it. She...inspired him in a way no other woman had. It wasn't just an attraction; it was more. She didn't want anything from him. Unlike the sharks circling around the Rowling ballroom, Serafia didn't need his money and she certainly didn't want to share his spotlight. He felt that she was someone he could trust, especially after she shared her own story with him. Her past was different from his but he could tell that it had scarred her in a similar way. The difference was that he didn't trust others and she didn't trust herself. But she should. And he wanted to help her with that.

It made her ever more attractive to him, if that was possible. She wasn't just the supermodel from his teenage fantasies. She was so much more. He just had to convince her of that.

"The car is slowing down," Serafia noted. She climbed from his lap and quickly started pulling herself back together.

Gabriel turned and looked out the window. They were approaching the gate to the compound. "We're home. Time to get dressed so we can go inside and I can take it all off you again."

Serafia tugged the top of her dress back up over her shoulders and looked at him. "Really?"

How silly she was to doubt him on that point. "Oh yes," Gabriel said in a tone as serious as he was capable of. "That was just to hold me over until we got home."

Seven

Serafia woke up the next morning with a small smile on her lips. Opening her eyes, she spied Gabriel's broad shoulders as he slept beside her. She rolled onto her back with a yawn and reached for her phone to check the time. It was eight-thirty, practically midday for her. She wasn't surprised, considering that Gabriel hadn't let her sleep until after three.

Flinging back the sheets, she gently slipped out of the bed so she wouldn't wake Gabriel. She snatched up a blanket off the foot of the bed, wrapped it around her naked body and walked toward the wall of French doors that led from the master bedroom onto a secluded patio that overlooked the sea.

She stepped out onto the balcony, pulling the door shut behind her. The sun was bright, warming her skin as she took in the remarkable view.

Playa del Onda was built on a sheer cliff overlooking the sea. It was perched at the apex of a crescent-shaped bay lined with sailboats and beaches that would hopefully draw tourists now that the Tantaberras had fallen. The water was an enchanting mix of blues and greens that begged you to dip a toe into it. It reminded her of her hacienda in Barcelona. Her view overlooked the Mediterranean, but the feelings it inspired in her were the same. Peacefulness. The ability to breathe. Relaxation.

She wanted to take a mug of coffee and sit out here the rest of the morning, but that just wasn't possible. The house was crawling with guards and servants. She couldn't stroll into the kitchen wearing a blanket and slip back into the prince's suite without someone noticing. Not that it was necessarily a secret to those who'd traveled back to the beach house with them last night, but she thought it was inappropriate to flaunt it.

As it was, she needed to get down the hall to her own room. Going back inside, she checked to see that Gabriel was still asleep. She had worked wonders with his transformation, but bless him, he was still a night owl.

She retrieved her gown from the floor and slipped it back on, and then slowly opened the door of his bedroom, glancing both ways down the hall to see if anyone was there. The coast was clear. She slipped out, pulling the door closed. She had taken about three steps toward her room when she heard something behind her.

"Good morning, Señorita Espina."

She turned to find the houseman, Luca, standing behind her. "Good morning, Luca," she said, self-consciously smoothing her hand over her tousled hair and trying to downplay how over-dressed she was for the early morning hours.

His dark gaze traveled over her quickly, a twinkle of amusement in his eyes, but he didn't mention her appearance. "Is His Majesty still sleeping?" he asked.

"Yes, he is. But he should be getting up soon. Please wake him by ten if he hasn't roused by then."

"As you wish."

Serafia started to turn back toward her room, and then she stopped. "Please don't mention this to anyone," she said.

Luca shook his head. "Of course not, señorita. The affairs of the prince are no one's concern but the prince's. But..." He hesitated. "You should know your involvement with the prince is no secret."

Serafia looked up at him with eyes wide with panic. "What does that mean?"

He unfolded the Alma newspaper he'd been clutching in his hand and held it up for her to read. On the front page, just below the article about Gabriel's big introduction at the Rowling party, was a headline that read *"The Future Queen?"* Another article followed, speculating about a romance brewing between her and

Gabriel. A grainy black-and-white photo of them kissing by the fountain accompanied the story.

With a sigh, she closed her eyes. She felt foolish for thinking she could have one moment of privacy. "Thank you for showing me this, Luca. May I take it to my room and read it?"

He folded the paper and handed it to her. "Of course."

Serafia tucked it under her arm. "Please don't mention it to the prince until I have a chance to read the article. I'll discuss it with him at breakfast."

"As you wish. I'll have Marta start preparing it."

Luca disappeared down the hallway, leaving Serafia with the newspaper clutched against her. Before anyone else saw her, she dashed down the hallway to her own room.

Throwing the paper onto the bed, she headed straight for the shower. As the steaming hot water pounded her sore muscles and washed away Gabriel's scent from her skin, her mind started to race with the implications of the article. From what little she'd read, the tone didn't seem negative. The prince and his quest for a bride would be front page news no matter who he was seen with. But that didn't do much to calm her anxiety.

She should've known better than to think that someone hadn't noticed their departure from the ballroom and followed them outside. She hadn't noticed anyone there, but with the walls of hedges and arborvitae columns, there were plenty of places to hide and spy on their painfully private moments together.

Hopefully whoever took their picture hadn't been able to hear their conversation over the sound of the nearby fountain. The photo was one thing, but she didn't want the revelations about her departure from modeling to taint Gabriel somehow.

Stepping from the shower, Serafia wrapped herself in a fluffy white towel and started combing through the thick and easily tangled strands of her hair. She rushed through the rest of her morning routine. Trying to maintain a bit of professionalism, she put her hair up in a tight bun and dressed in a dark plum pantsuit. They had another official event to attend this afternoon, so she might as well get ready and put her consultant hat back on.

After she slipped on her shoes, she reached for the paper and read through both articles on Gabriel. The first, about his introduction at the Rowling party, was extremely positive. The consensus was that he was well received and those in attendance were pleased to have such a fine man to be their future king.

The second article, about her, wasn't really bad, either. It discussed the various ladies he had danced with that night, highlighting Helena Ruiz as his first choice and Serafia as his last. Of course, there was the photo of them kissing, and then a lot of speculation about whether or not she was really his social secretary, or if it was a cover for their relationship. If they were dating, was it serious? Might she be their new queen? The few people they interviewed for the article seemed to think she'd make a good candidate for queen of Alma and would make a charming match for Gabriel.

It wasn't a horrible write-up, but she really wished she could have avoided the papers. How could he turn around and select one of the other women in Alma after this? No one wanted to be second choice and really, she wasn't in the running to be queen, despite what they might think.

Or was she?

Gabriel seemed as serious about her as he had been about anything they'd discussed so far. He'd swept her off her feet and for once, she'd gone with it and had an amazing night. She hadn't entertained second thoughts about it, but now anxiety started pooling in her stomach. She wasn't opposed to being his lover, but queen? She wasn't sure she could handle that. The only people more famous in Europe than models were the royal families. The United Kingdom's Princess Kate couldn't wear an unflattering dress or have a bad hair day without it being in the papers and commented on. Every time Prince Harry was seen with a woman, the rumors would fly.

Serafia knew what it was like. In her modeling days, it wasn't enough for everyone to critique her appearance, and they did. Her whole life was public. The cameras showed up on dates, on vacations, while she was trying to spend a day with her family. If she was dating anyone famous, the magnifying glass tripled along with the coverage. It was incredibly difficult to maintain a relationship under the microscope, much less a shred of self-esteem.

It had nearly killed her to do it, but Serafia had escaped the spotlight. Gabriel's queen would be subject to the same kind of scrutiny. The private would become painfully public, with every aspect of her life exposed. She had no intention of ever going back in front of the cameras.

Even for Gabriel. Even for the chance to be queen. She would be much happier in Barcelona, living a quiet, unexciting life. Passionless, yes, but private.

With a sigh, she folded up the paper and headed out to breakfast. By the time she reached the dining hall, Gabriel was dressed and waiting for her there. Without her standing by the closet, laying out his clothes, he'd opted for a pair of jeans and a clingy green T-shirt that matched his eyes. His hair was still wet and slicked back, his cheeks still slightly pink from his shave. He was sipping a cup of coffee and thumbing through emails on his smart phone.

"Good morning," she said as she entered the room. She had her tablet in one hand and the newspaper in the other.

Gabriel smiled wide when he looked up at her. There was a wicked light in his eyes. "Good morning."

Serafia took a seat at the table across from him, holding off their discussion as Marta poured her a cup of coffee and returned to the kitchen to bring out their breakfast. They were three bites into their *tortilla de patatas* before she spoke about it.

"Apparently," she began, "we were not the

only people out in the garden last night. Our kiss made the front page of the newspaper." She laid the paper out on the table for Gabriel to look at it.

He picked it up, reading over the article as he chewed his eggs, a thoughtful expression on his face. "I'm not surprised," he said at last, dropping the paper on the table and returning to his breakfast. He didn't seem remotely concerned.

"It doesn't bother you?" she asked.

"This isn't my first romance documented in a gossip column. Nor is it yours, I'd wager. There's nothing inflammatory about it, so why should I care? You're not a dark secret I'm trying to hide."

"The press scrutiny will be higher now. They'll question every moment we're together. We'll need to meet with your press secretary, Hector, to discuss how to handle it."

"I know how we'll handle it," he said, sipping his orange juice. "The palace will not comment on the personal life of the prince. Period. If and when I select a queen, I will announce it through the proper channels, not through some gossip column. They can speculate all they like. It doesn't concern me."

Serafia sat back in her chair. She was near speechless. That was the most tactful and diplomatic thing he could've said on the subject. Maybe her lessons were finally sinking in. "That is an excellent answer. I'll make sure Hector knows that's the official position of the palace."

After a few minutes of silent eating, Gabriel put down his fork and looked at her. "What do you think about the article? You seemed to be more concerned about it than I am. Am I missing something?"

"No, it's not the content of the article itself, so much as being in it. I've lived happily out of the spotlight for years," she explained. "Finding myself back in the papers was…unnerving to say the least."

"Do you regret last night?" he asked.

Serafia's gaze lifted to meet his. "No. But I regret not being smarter about it."

Gabriel nodded and speared a bite of tortilla with his fork. "Good. Then we can do it again."

Lord, but Gabriel was hot. He would've been much more comfortable in the jeans and T-shirt he'd started the day in, but Serafia had made him change before they left Playa del Onda. Did Serafia give no thought when she selected his wardrobe that he would be touring the countryside of Alma in July? The vineyards were beautiful, and he really was interested in everything Tomás was telling him, but it was hard to focus when he could feel his back sweating under his suit coat.

As they walked through the arbors, he turned to look at Serafia. She had her hair up in a bun off her neck. She was wearing a wide-brimmed hat and a linen shift dress in a light green that looked infinitely cooler than his own suit.

"I'm dying here," he whispered, leaning into Serafia's ear. "I'm no good to anyone if I melt into a puddle."

"We're going inside in a minute."

Gabriel sighed. "We better be or I'm going to look terrible if the press take any more photos." There was a small group invited to the vineyard today. They'd taken some shots as he arrived and as they toured the fields and sampled grapes from the vines, but they had given him some space after that. They were probably hot, too, and waiting for the group to return to the air-conditioned comfort of the building.

"Such a warm day!" Tomás declared. "Let's head inside. I'll give you a tour of the wine cave, and then we'll get to the good part and sample my wares."

Gabriel's ears perked up at the mention of a wine cellar. He was happy to go inside, but that didn't sound like a place he was interested in visiting. "Did he say 'cave'?" he asked as they trekked back up the hill to the villa.

Serafia frowned at him. "Yes. Why?"

"I don't like going underground."

"I'm sure it will be fine. Just relax," she insisted. "We really need a nice, uneventful visit today."

Gabriel snorted. She was optimistic to a fault. "Do you actually think that's ever going to happen with me as the king?"

She tipped her head up to look at him from under the wide brim of her white-and-green hat. Her nose wrinkled delicately as she said, "Probably not, but I'll keep striving for it. Before long, I'll be turning you over to your staff and going home. I hope they're prepared."

They finally reached the top of the hill and stepped through the large doors of the warehouse. Inside, they were greeted by a servant with a tray of sparkling water and a bowl with cool towels.

"Please, take a minute to cool off," Tomás said. "Have you enjoyed the tour so far?"

"It's been lovely, Tomás. There's no doubt that this is the finest vineyard in Alma," Serafia said, sipping her water.

She must not have trusted Gabriel to say the right thing. "It's a beautiful property," he chimed in. "How many acres do you have here?"

"About two hundred. It's been in my family for ten generations."

"You withstood all the political upheaval?"

Gabriel felt Serafia tense beside him. He supposed it was impolite to ask the residents of Alma how they managed to cope with the dictatorship, but he was curious. Some fled, but most made the best of it somehow.

"My great-grandfather refused to abandon his family's home. It was that simple. To survive, we supplied our finest wines to the Tantaberras and were forced to pay their heavy commercial taxes, but we survived better than others. We had a commodity he wanted."

Lucky. Gabriel sipped the last of his water and after dabbing his neck and forehead, returned the cloth to the bowl. "And now?"

Tomás smiled brightly. "Much better, Your Grace. Now we are finally able to export our wines to Europe and America. Before, we were restricted by heavy trade embargos that punished us more than the dictatorship. The free trade of the last few months has had a huge impact on our sales and profits. We were able to hire more staff and plant more grapes this year than ever before. We are prospering."

Gabriel smiled. He had nothing to do with the changes, but he was happy to see them. Serafia had impressed upon him how hard it had been on his people since the Montoros left. He was glad to see the course reverse so quickly with the Tantaberras gone.

"Are we ready to continue?"

Gabriel was not, but he followed behind Tomás, anyway. A few of the journalists joined them as they walked through the warehouse to a heavy oak door. Tomás went down first with a few others, leaving Gabriel standing at the top of the stairs with a sense of dread pooling in his stomach. His hands clutched the railing, but his feet refused to take another step.

"Go!" Serafia urged him from behind.

He could see Tomás standing at the bottom of the stairs waiting for him with a few reporters. The light was dim and the air cool. Their host had an expectant look on his face as he stood there waiting for Gabriel to follow.

Serafia nudged him in the back with her knee and he took a few steps down without really wanting to. It was only two more steps to the bottom, so he forced himself to go the rest of the way down. At the very least he needed to keep going so that the ladder would be clear for his escape. Right now Serafia, a vineyard assistant and a few other reporters were behind him.

Gabriel took a labored breath and looked around him. The room was bigger than he'd expected. The long corridor with its arched ceiling stretched on for quite a distance. Dim gold lights were spaced out down the hall, providing enough light to see the hundreds of barrels stored there.

The air was also fresher than he'd anticipated. He looked up, spying air vents that led to some type of ventilation system. At least the room didn't smell of stale bread and mildew. But it didn't need to. Gabriel's brain easily conjured those smells. Dank, musty air filled his lungs, tainted with the stench of his own waste and leftover food that was rotting in the corner of his prison.

"This is my pride and joy," Tomás said, taking a few steps down the rows of barrels. "This is a natural cave my family found on the property. It was perfect for storing our wine barrels, so we didn't have to build a separate cellar. My great-grandfather added the electrical lighting and ventilation system so we can maintain the perfect temperature and humidity for the wine."

He continued to talk, but Gabriel couldn't hear him. All he could hear was his own heartbeat pounding in his ears. There were no windows, no natural light. He hated that. He couldn't even stand his room at the palace with the dim light and cavelike conditions.

It was all too much. He could feel the walls start to close in on him. He could feel the rope chafing his ankles. Beads of perspiration that had nothing to do with heat formed on his brow and on his palms. He rubbed his hands absently against the fabric of his light gray suit, but it didn't help. They were starting to tremble.

"We have nearly five hundred barrels—"

"I have to go!" Gabriel announced, interrupting Tomás and pushing through the crowd to reach the staircase. He ignored the commotion around him, taking the steps two at a time until he reached the ground floor.

There, he could finally take a breath. Bending over, he clasped his knees and closed his eyes. He breathed slowly, willing his heart rate to drop and his muscles to unwind. He stood upright and turned when he heard the stampede of footsteps coming up the steps behind him.

"Your Majesty, are you well?" Tomás approached him, placing a cautious hand on his shoulder.

Gabriel raised his arm to dismiss his concerns. "I'm fine. I'm sorry about that. I don't do well in closed in spaces."

"I wish I had known. I would never have taken you down there. Señorita Espina didn't mention it."

"She didn't know." Not really. He'd explained about his kidnapping the night before, but he hadn't expressed how much things like small spaces or wrist watches bothered him as a result. He didn't like talking about it. To him, it felt like a weakness. Kings weren't supposed to have panic attacks. He didn't mind being flawed, but he hated for anyone, and especially Serafia, to think of him as weak.

"Gabriel, are you okay?" Serafia asked, coming to his side with concern pinching her brow.

"I just needed some air. Sorry, everyone, the heat must've gotten to me," he said more loudly to the crowd that followed him.

"I think what you need is a seat on the veranda with some wine and food to reinforce you," Tomás suggested.

They followed the crowd into the villa, but before they entered, Serafia tugged at his jacket and held him back. "What was all that about?" she asked once they were alone.

As much as he hated to tell her, he needed to. He couldn't have another incident like this. "I've developed a sort of claustrophobia since my kidnapping. I can't take small or dark spaces, especially underground ones like the room where I was kept. I have panic attacks. It's the same with watches. I can't bear the feel of things against my wrists."

Serafia sighed and brought her hand to his cheek. "Why didn't you tell me?"

Gabriel covered her hand with his own and pulled it down to his chest. When he looked into her dark brown eyes, he felt overcome with the urge to tell her whatever she wanted. He wanted to be honest with someone for the first time since he came home from Venezuela. Serafia was the one person he could trust with his secrets.

"Because I've never told anyone."

Eight

Serafia got up early the next morning, slipping from Gabriel's bed to get ready. An hour later she returned and started sifting through his clothes for the perfect outfit.

"It's seven-thirty," he groaned as he sat up in bed. His hair was tousled and as the sheets pooled around his waist, Serafia couldn't help stealing a glance at the hard muscles she'd become accustomed to touching each night. "Why are you up so early clinking wooden hangers together?"

With a sigh, she turned back to the closet.

"I'm trying to figure out what you should wear today for the parade."

"I'm going to be in a parade?"

It was becoming clear to her that in the early days of working together, Gabriel had paid very little attention to what she'd said. The prime minister's office had arranged for a full week of activities and Gabriel had been briefed on them in detail while they were still in Miami. And yet each day was like a surprise for him.

After the incident at the vineyard, Serafia was afraid to know if Gabriel had a problem with parades, too. She didn't dare ask. "Yes. As we discussed in Miami," she emphasized, "they're holding a welcome parade for you this morning that will go through the capital of Del Sol."

"Are there going to be marching bands and floats or something?"

"No, it's not really that kind of parade." She pulled out a gray pin-striped suit coat. It would be too hot for his ceremonial attire and that was better saved for the coronation parade, anyway. A nice suit would be just right, she thought.

Eyeing the ties, she pondered which would look best. She knew Gabriel would be more inclined to skip the tie, but that wouldn't look right. She frowned at the closet. The more she got to know Gabriel, the more she realized she was trying to force him into a box he didn't really fit in, but he was still royalty and needed to dress appropriately.

"People are just going to stand out on the sidewalk and wait for me to come by and wave? Like the pope?"

Serafia looked at him with exasperation and planted her hands on her hips. "You're going to be the king! Yes. People want to see you, even if it's just for a moment as you drive by and wave. It won't be as big as your formal coronation parade, but it gives everyone in Alma the chance to come and see you, not just the press or the rich people at Patrick Rowling's party."

"For their sake, I hope there are at least vendors out there selling some good street food," he muttered as he climbed out of bed.

"Get in the shower," Serafia said, laying the suit out across the bed.

Gabriel came up behind her and pulled her into his arms, crushing her back against his bare body. "Wanna get in there with me?" his low voice grumbled into her ear.

Serafia felt a thrill rush through her body, but she fought the reaction. They didn't have time for this now, as much as she'd like to indulge. There were thousands of people already lining the streets in the hopes of getting a good spot to see Gabriel. She turned in his arms and kissed him, then quickly pulled away. "Sorry, but you're going it alone today," she said. "We leave in less than an hour."

She was amazed they were able to keep to their schedule, but everything went to plan. They rendezvoused with the rest of the motorcade a few miles away from the advertised route. Gabriel was transferred to a convertible where he could sit on the top of the backseats and wave to the crowd. Royal guards and Del

Sol police would be driving ahead of his car and behind, with guards running alongside them.

"Remember," Serafia said as he got settled in the back of the car. "Smile, wave, be sure to turn to look at both sides of the street. People are excited to see you. Be excited to see them, too, and you'll win the hearts of your people. I'll see you at the end of the route."

"I thought you might ride with me."

Serafia shook her head. "You're Prince Gabriel, soon to be King Gabriel. As far as anyone else knows, I'm your social secretary. Social secretaries wouldn't ride along on something like this. We don't need to give the newspapers any more material to put into their gossip columns. So no, I'm not going with you. You'll do fine."

Ignoring nearly everything she'd just said, he leaned in and gave her a kiss in front of fifty witnesses. Hopefully none of them had cameras. "See you on the flip side," he said.

Serafia shook her head and climbed into another car that was driving ahead to ensure that the route was clear and to secure the end rendezvous location.

Looking out the window, she was impressed by how many people were lining the streets. Thousands of people from all over, young and old alike, had come to the capital to see Gabriel. Some held signs of welcome; others had white carnations, the official flower of Alma, to throw into the street in front of Gabriel's car. Their faces lit up with excitement and anticipation as they saw Serafia's official palace vehicle drive down the road, indicating that the new king would soon follow.

They needed a reason to smile. The Tantaberras had ruled over these people with an iron fist for too long. They deserved freedom and hope, and she sincerely believed that Gabriel could be the one to bring it to them. He wasn't the most traditional choice for a king, but he was a good man. He was caring and thoughtful. There might be a rocky start, but she could tell these people were desperate for the excitement of a new king, a new queen and the kind of royal baby countdown that the British had recently enjoyed.

Serafia spied a different sign as they neared the end of the route. A little girl was holding up a board with Gabriel's picture and her own. Across the top and bottom in blue glitter it read "We need a fairy tale romance! King Gabriel & Queen Serafia forever!"

A few feet down, another declared "We have our king, please choose Serafia as our queen!" This one was held by an older woman. A third declared "Unite the Montoros & the Espinas at last!"

Serafia sat back in her seat in surprise. Although she preferred to avoid the press in general, the tone of the earlier article about her and Gabriel had been positive. The crowd here today seemed to corroborate that. They had their king and now they wanted their fairy tale. But her? Serafia didn't need to be anyone's queen. She was done with the spotlight.

The only hitch was her growing feelings for Gabriel. She'd never planned them. If she was honest, she hadn't wanted to have feelings for him at all. And yet, over the last two weeks, he had charmed his way into her heart. She wasn't in love, but she was closer than she'd been in a very long time. Her time with Gabriel was coming to an end. Soon he would be on his own, transitioning into his role as king. Serafia planned to return to Barcelona when it was over.

But as the time ticked away, she felt herself dreading that day. What was her alternative? To stay? To let her relationship with Gabriel grow into something real? That would give the people of Alma what they wanted, but it came at too high a price. Serafia didn't want to be queen. She was done with the criticism and the magnifying glass examining her every decision and action.

The car stopped at a park and she got out, waiting with a small crew of guards and Hector Vega, who was speaking to some journalists. She found a spot in the shade where she could lean against one of the vehicles and wait for the royal motorcade. It wasn't in sight yet, so she glanced down to pull out her tablet to make some notes.

"Serafia?"

She looked up at the sound of a woman's voice and noticed Felicia Gomez and her daughter crossing the street to speak with her. The older woman had traded her ball gown for a more casual blouse and slacks, but she was wearing almost as many diamonds. She was smiling as much as her Botox would allow, but there wasn't much sincerity in the look. Dita was wearing a sundress and a fresh-faced look guaranteed to turn Gabriel's head.

Serafia swallowed her negative observations and tried to smile with more warmth than she had. "Señora Gomez, Dita. Good morning. How are you?"

"I'm well," Felicia replied, coming to stand beside her. "We came down in the hopes we'd get a chance to speak with the prince after the parade. We didn't get a lot of time at the Rowling party."

Felicia's tone was pointed, as though Serafia were the one responsible for that fact. In a way she was, she supposed. Serafia didn't want the crown, but she really didn't want the spoiled Dita to have it, either.

Instead of responding, Serafia just smiled and turned to look down the street. She could see the motorcycle cops leading the motorcade. "Here's your opportunity," she said.

Within a few minutes, all the vehicles had pulled into the park. Gabriel leaped out of the back of the convertible with athletic grace. He shook the hands of his driver and the guards who were running along with him, and then made his way over to Serafia. He was smiling as he looked at her, barely paying any attention to the Gomez women standing beside her.

"I'm starving," he said. "All that waving and smiling has worked up a hellacious appetite. I caught a whiff of something delicious on the parade route. I think it was coming from this little tapas place. I tried to remember the landmarks and I'm determined to track it down for lunch."

"That's fine, we're almost done here."

"What else do I have to do?" he asked.

Serafia shifted her gaze toward the two expectant women beside her without turning her head. Gabriel followed the movement and put on his practiced smile when he noticed who it was. She'd taught him well, it seemed. "Señora and Señorita Gomez have been waiting for you."

"Your Grace," Felicia said as both she and Dita gave a brief curtsey. "We'd hoped to have a moment of your time after the parade. The party had simply too many people for us to have a proper conversation."

That translated to: *You didn't spend enough time with my daughter and if she's going to be queen, she needs time to work her charms on you.*

"Are you hungry?" he asked.

Felicia seemed a little taken aback. "Hungry, Your Grace?"

"I was just telling Señorita Espina that I spied the most delicious-smelling tapas restaurant. It looks like a hole in the wall, but I'm anxious to try it. Would you care to join us?"

Serafia could see the conflict in Felicia's eyes. The Gomez family wasn't one to be seen at a run-down tapas restaurant. Serafia fought to hold in a twitter of laughter as she watched the older woman choose between two unpleasant fates—dining with commoners and being turned away by the prince once again. There was a pained expression on her face as she finally responded.

"That is very kind of Your Grace. We have already eaten, unfortunately. But perhaps you would give us the honor of hosting you at our home for dinner sometime soon."

"That's a very kind offer. I'll see when I can take you up on it. It was good to see you both again. Señora Gomez. Señorita Gomez," he said, tipping his head to each in turn. "Have a lovely afternoon."

At that, he smiled and put his arm around

Serafia's shoulder. Together, they made their way from the disgruntled Gomez women over to his private car to track down some tasty tapas.

Serafia waited until the car door was shut and the tinted windows blocked them from sight, and then burst out laughing. "Did you see the look on her face when you invited her to go get some lunch? I nearly dislocated a rib trying not to laugh."

"Did I handle it okay?"

"You did very well. It isn't your fault she won't stoop to the level of an average person. She isn't going to give up, though. She wants you to marry Dita and she'll keep trying until you do."

Gabriel looked at her in a way that made her bones turn to melted butter. "She can *try*," he said. "But I'll be the one with the crown on my head. I make the decisions when it comes to who I date and who I'll marry."

Serafia felt her heart stutter in her chest as he spoke the words, looking intently at her. She knew in that moment that she needed to be very, very careful if she didn't want the crown of Alma on her head, as well.

The following morning, Gabriel decided he wanted to take his breakfast out on the patio overlooking the sea. The weather was beautiful, the skies were blue and the fresh sea air reminded him of home.

Sitting in the shade of the veranda, he sipped the coffee Luca brought him and watched a sailboat slip across the bay. How long had it been since he'd gone sailing? Too long. Once this coronation business was over and he could settle into being king, he intended to remedy that.

He could just picture Serafia standing on the deck, clutching the railing and watching the water as they cut through the waves. He imagined her wearing nothing but a pair of linen shorts hugging the curve of her rear and a bikini top tied around her neck. Her golden skin would darken in the sun, her long dark hair blowing in the sea breeze.

That sounded like heaven. It made him wonder if there was already a boat in the possession of the royal family. If there was, he'd ensure that they took it out for a spin as soon as possible.

As he took another sip, Luca appeared in the doorway. "Luca, do you know if we have a boat?"

"A boat, Your Grace?"

"Yes. We have a beach house. Do we have a boat?"

"Yes, there is a sailboat at the marina. The youngest Tantaberra was an avid sailor."

At the marina. Perhaps they could go out sooner than later. When he looked back at Luca, he realized he had the Alma newspaper in his hand. "Is that today's paper?" he asked.

Judging by the concerned expression on Luca's face, the latest royal coverage was not as positive as he'd hoped. He imagined the press had had a field day ragging on him about that panic attack at the vineyard. It wasn't the most kingly thing he'd done this week. He'd thought the parade went alright, though.

Gabriel frowned as he looked at Luca. "That good, eh? Should I go ahead and call Hector?"

"Señor Vega already knows, Your Grace. Ernesto called a moment ago to let me know that Señor Vega was already on his way here to speak with you."

Great. Gabriel would much rather use his spare time to get acquainted with every square inch of Serafia's body, but instead he would be discussing damage-control strategies with his high-strung press secretary. He had only met Hector a few times, and that was enough. The man consumed entirely too much caffeine. At least, Gabriel hoped he did. If the man was naturally that spun-up, he felt bad for the mother who'd had to chase him around as a toddler.

Hector made him anxious. Serafia made him calm. He knew exactly who he preferred to work with. He had to convince her to stay beyond the end of the week, be it as a paid employee or as his girlfriend.

"Let me see the damage before he gets here," Gabriel said, reaching out for the paper. "It must be bad if Hector immediately hopped in his car."

Gabriel glanced at the headlines, expecting the story to be about him, but instead he found a scathing story about the Espina family. He looked up at Luca. "Have you told Miss Espina about this, yet?"

"No, sir, but she should be down for breakfast momentarily. Would you like me to warn her?"

"No, I'll tell her."

Maybe they could have a game plan before Hector arrived and started spinning.

Turning back to the article, he started reading it in depth. Apparently, back when the coup took place in the 1940s, there were rumors about the loyalty of the Espina family. He hadn't heard that before. Surely if there had been any legitimacy to that claim, their families wouldn't have vacationed together and his father wouldn't have allowed Serafia to work with him these past few weeks.

Of course, his father had been quite curt where Serafia was concerned. He'd alluded to her family being unsuitable somehow, but Gabriel hadn't had a moment alone with his father to press him on that point. He was sure it was nothing to do with Serafia herself. Gabriel had chalked up his father's bad mood to jealousy. That was the most likely reason for his behavior since they arrived in Alma.

"Good morning." Serafia slipped out onto the patio in a pair of black capris and a sleeveless top. Her dark hair was swept up into a ponytail and she was wearing bejeweled sandals instead of dress pumps. They didn't have any official events on the calendar today, so she had apparently dressed for a more casual afternoon by the sea.

"Hector is on his way," he replied, not mincing words.

Serafia's smile faded and she slipped down into the other chair. "What happened?"

"Apparently the newspaper headlines have gone from speculating about your role as future queen to speculating about your family's role in the overthrow of the Montoros."

Serafia's eyebrows drew together in concern as she reached for the paper. "What are they talking about?" Her gaze flicked over the paper. "This is ridiculous. Our families aren't enemies and we most certainly didn't have anything do with the coup. Have they forgotten that the Espinas were driven from Alma, too? They lived in Switzerland for years until the dictatorship fell in Spain. I was born in Madrid just a few years after they left Switzerland."

Gabriel shrugged. "I am deficient in Alman history. We should probably fix that. I didn't even have a clue our families had been rivals for the throne at one point."

"That was over a hundred years ago. How is that even relevant to what's going on now?"

"It has everything to do with what's happening now," Hector Vega said, appearing in the doorway and butting into their conversation. He, too, had the newspaper under his arm. "Your family had the crown stolen away from them two hundred years ago. The Espinas and Montoros fought for years to seize control of these islands. The Montoros ended up winning and eventually the families did reconcile. They even planned to marry and combine the bloodlines.

"But," he continued ominously, "Rafael the First broke off his engagement with Rosa Espina to marry Anna Maria. There were more than a few hurt feelings about that and plenty of rumors went around during the time of the coup about the Espinas' involvement. Your whole family vanished from Alma right before everything fell apart. Some see that as suspicious."

"And now?" Serafia pressed. "I think my family has gotten over the embarrassment of a broken engagement during the last seventy years. There is no reason to suspect us of anything."

"Isn't there? With the Tantaberras gone and the Montoros returning to Alma, your family is closer to reclaiming their throne than ever before," Hector explained.

"How?" Gabriel asked. "By marrying me? That plan only works if I'm on board with it."

Hector shrugged. "That's one way to do it." He moved out onto the veranda with them, but instead of taking a chair, he started pacing back and forth across the terra-cotta tiles of the patio. "Another way is to remove the Montoros entirely. If the Montoros and the Salazars were scandalized or discredited, Senorita Espina's family would be the next in line."

Gabriel had no idea that was the case, and judging by the surprised drop of Serafia's jaw, she didn't know it, either. "But there are several of us in line. They'd have to discredit us all, not just me."

"There are fewer of you than you think. Your father and brother have already been put aside. That just leaves you, Bella and Juan Carlos. Don't think it can't be done."

"There is no way that Juan Carlos can be discredited by scandal," Gabriel insisted. "He's annoyingly perfect."

"It doesn't matter," Hector said. "That article insinuates that Serafia was deliberately planted within the royal family to undermine you from the inside."

"She's here to help me!" Gabriel shouted. He

was irritated that this stupidity had ruined a perfectly beautiful morning.

"Is she?" Hector stopped moving just long enough to look over Serafia with suspicion.

"Of course I am. How dare you suggest otherwise?" Serafia flushed bright red beneath her tanned glow.

Hector raised his hands in defeat. "Fine. Fine. But the accusations are out there. We have to figure out how we're going to address them."

"They're ridiculous," Gabriel said. "I don't even want to address the rumors. At least not yet. It could all blow over if we treat it like the unfounded gossip it is."

Hector nodded and stopped pacing long enough to take notes in the small notebook he had tucked into his breast pocket.

"I just don't understand," Serafia said. "The press was so positive toward our relationship just a day ago. What changed so quickly?"

Hector put his notebook away and turned to look out at the sea, his fingers tapping anxiously on the railing. "My guess would be that someone leaked the story to discredit Serafia."

"Why?" Gabriel asked. "What could she have done to anger someone so quickly?"

Hector's gaze ran over Serafia with his lips pressed together tightly. "She didn't do anything. My guess is that it was your doing. You rejected the daughters of all the wealthiest families at the Rowling party."

Gabriel rolled his eyes. "Even if I hadn't left that night with Serafia—which really means nothing, since she's staying here with me for work—only one woman can be chosen as queen. There were easily twenty or thirty girls there that night. How could I possibly choose without offending *someone*?"

"It bet it was Felicia Gomez," Serafia said, speaking up. "Yesterday's incident just compounded their irritation over the party. The Gomez family doesn't like to lose and as I recall, you didn't even dance with Dita that night. I imagine Felicia would see that as a major snub. Combine that with yesterday after the parade…

I'm sure they ran right to the press after we left. She can't take it out on you, as king, so she focused her ire on their main competition—me."

Gabriel muffled a snort and shook his head. "They wouldn't go to this much trouble if they knew the truth."

"What's the truth?" Serafia asked.

Gabriel looked into her dark eyes with a serious expression. "They're hardly your competition."

Nine

"How, exactly, did you come up with a boat?" Serafia asked as she turned to Gabriel.

Gabriel looked up from the wheel of the yacht and grinned. After a morning of unpleasantness with Hector, he'd had Luca arrange for the boat to go out. He needed to escape, to think, and there was nothing better than the sea for that.

Marta had packed them a picnic basket so they could dine on the water. The sea was calm and the breeze was just strong enough to fill the sails and keep them from getting too hot. "Turns out it's mine," he said. "Or at least it is now. I thought it was a good day to be out on the water."

"To escape the press?" she asked.

He chuckled and shook his head. "That's just a bonus. Mainly I wanted to see you in a bikini."

Serafia smiled and held out her arms to display her mostly bare curves. She was wearing a bright blue-and-pink paisley bikini top with a pair of tiny denim shorts that made her legs look as if they went on for miles. He ached to touch them, but he needed to steer the boat.

"You got your wish," she declared.

"Indeed I did." The reality standing in front of him was even better than he'd imagined this morning.

"If they know we're out here, the paparazzi will follow us, you know."

"Then they'll get an eyeful and the pictures will leave no doubts that their seedy story made no impact on my opinion of you."

He focused on steering the boat out of the sheltered bay and into open water as she laid a beach towel down on the polished wooden deck. She slipped out of the tiny shorts and went about rubbing sunblock all over her golden skin.

Thank goodness there weren't many ships out on the water today. His eyes were so glued to her that he could've run aground or rammed another boat. He couldn't wait to find a good place to stop so he could join her on the deck.

Serafia glanced up at him and smiled. She looked beautiful and carefree for once; she'd even left her tablet behind today. Not at all like someone scheming her way into his life, he thought, as the events from the morning intruded on his admiration of her. The whole thing was just absurd. Their families might have had animosity a hundred years ago, but that wasn't the case now. The people involved in that were long dead. It didn't have a thing to do with him or Serafia.

The idea that she had been "planted" in his inner circle to undermine him made his hands curl into fists at his side. Serafia hadn't been *planted* anywhere. He had hired her. She hadn't even suggested the idea; in fact, she'd been very reluctant to take the job. If she was here to lure him into bed, she'd certainly made it difficult. He'd worked harder on her seduction than he had in a long time.

As much as he wanted to just laugh off the story, he couldn't. It made him too angry. He wouldn't tolerate such ugly speculation, especially about Serafia or her family. He'd quietly tasked Hector with tracking down the author of the article and seeing if the source could be identified. If the Gomez family really was behind this story, they'd regret it. If they thought his snubbing Dita at the dance was a huge deal, they'd better be prepared to be shut out of his court entirely. Gabriel was able to carry grudges for a very long time. He wouldn't quickly forget about the people who tried to undermine his faith in the one person he trusted.

Everyone had seen that article. Not long after Hector left, Gabriel's father had called from Del Sol. Rafael was agitated about the whole thing, repeating what he'd said at the Rowling party about the Espinas. Since this time they weren't in public where they could be overheard, Gabriel had pushed his father for more information. Arturo Espina was one of his father's best friends. How could he turn around and be suspicious of the family?

Rafael insisted it wasn't the truth that was the problem. It was seventy years of rumors that would taint his relationship with her. If he were to go as far as to make Serafia his queen, they would forever be dogged by those same ugly stories. Everyone had seen this article and it was just the beginning. Rafael insisted he was just trying to help Gabriel avoid all that. Being king was hard enough, he reasoned, without adding unnecessary complications.

If staying away from Serafia was the only way to save his reign from rumors, innuendo and scandal, too bad. He wasn't going to let something like this drive a wedge between them.

"It's so beautiful out here," Serafia declared, pulling him from his dark thoughts.

It was beautiful. The water was an amazing

mix of blues and greens; the sky was perfectly clear. Looking back to the shore, you could see the coastline dotted with marinas and tiny homes hanging on the side of the cliffs. He couldn't imagine a more amazing place to rule over.

Before too long, he would be king of this beautiful country.

From the moment he found out, he had fought the news. He'd made a bold decision to take control of his own life after his abduction, and yet somehow fate had taken away his free will once again. Most people would probably jump at the chance to be in his shoes, but all Gabriel had been able to see were all the reasons why he was a bad choice.

But now that he was here with Serafia at his side, it seemed as though things might work out. The people were welcoming and friendly. The land was beautiful and full of natural resources that would help the country bounce back from oppression. Prime Minister Rivera was a smart man and a good leader, taking the reins on the important decisions for the management of the country. The press were the press, but once he chose a queen and married, hopefully they would settle down.

Gabriel was told that he would soon sit down with his council of advisers, a group of staffers that included Hector and others. He was certain they would have lots of opinions about whom he should choose for his queen. There were geopolitical implications that even he didn't fully understand. Marrying a Spanish or Portuguese princess would be smart. Securing trade by marrying a Danish princess wouldn't hurt, either. Then there were the local wealthy citizens whose support was so important to the success of the new monarchy.

But factoring in all those things would mean he was following his head, not his heart. Gabriel wasn't exactly known for making the smart choices where women were concerned. When it came to Serafia, none of those other things mattered. The minute he saw her out on the patio in Miami, he'd wanted her. And the more he'd had of her, the more he'd wanted. He wasn't just flattering her when he told her the other women in Alma were no competition. It was the truth.

Serafia was smart, beautiful, honest, caring… everything a good queen should be. She was from an important Alman family—one with blood ties to the throne if that article could be believed. He saw more than one sign at the parade declaring the people's support for her as queen. She was a good choice on paper and a great choice in his heart.

He wasn't in love with Serafia. Not yet. But he could see the potential there. In any other scenario, he would've anticipated months or years together before they discussed love and marriage, but as king, he saw this as an entirely different animal. He was expected to make a choice and move forward. With Serafia, he had no fears that their marriage would be a stiff, arranged situation with an awkward honeymoon night. It could be the best of both worlds if they played their cards right.

He just had to get her to stay past the end of the week. If he could do that, then maybe, just maybe, she would agree to be his queen someday soon.

"This looks like a good spot. Drop the stupid anchor and get over here. I'm lonely."

Gabriel checked the depth sounder for a good location. They seemed to be in an area with a fairly level depth. He lowered and secured the two sails, slowing the boat. It took a few minutes to get the anchor lowered and set, but the boat finally came to a full stop.

He turned off any unnecessary equipment and made his way over to where Serafia was lying out. She was on her back, her inky black hair spilling across the sandy blond wood of the deck. She had her wide, dark sunglasses on, but the smile curling her lips indicated she was watching him as he admired her.

Gabriel dropped down onto the deck beside her. He slipped out of his shoes and pulled his polo shirt over his head, leaving on his swimming trunks.

Serafia sat up, grabbing her bottle of sunscreen and applying some to his back. He closed his eyes and enjoyed the feel of her hands gliding across his bare skin. After she finished his back and arms, she placed a playful dab on his nose and cheeks. "There you go."

He rubbed the last of the sunscreen into his face. "Thanks. Are you hungry?"

"Yes," she said. "After everything this morning, I couldn't stomach any breakfast."

Gabriel reached for the picnic basket and set it closer to them on the blanket. Opening it, they uncovered a container filled with assorted slices of aged Manchego and Cabrales cheeses, and cured meats like *jamón ibérico* and *cecina de León*. Smaller containers revealed olives, grapes and cherry tomatoes dressed in olive oil and sherry vinegar. A jar of quince jam, a couple fresh, sliced baguettes and a bottle of Spanish Cava rounded out the meal. His stomach started growling at the sight of it.

Serafia started unpacking the cartons, laying out the plates and utensils Marta had also included. "Ooh," she said, lifting out a package wrapped in foil. "This smells like cinnamon and sugar." She unwrapped a corner to peer inside. "Looks like fruit empanadas for dessert."

"Perfect," Gabriel said.

They scooped various items onto their plates and dug into their meals. They took their time enjoying every bite in the slow European fashion he was becoming accustomed to. In America, eating was like a pit stop in a race—to quickly refuel and get back on the track. Now, he took the time to savor the food, to really taste it while enjoying his company. He sliced bread while Serafia slathered it with jam. She fed him olives and kissed the olive oil from his lips. By the time the jars were nearly empty, they were both full and happy, lying on the deck together and gazing up at the brilliant blue sky.

Gabriel reached out beside him and felt for Serafia's hand. He wrapped his fingers through hers and felt a sense of calm and peace come over him. He didn't know what he would've done without her these last few days. In that short time, she had become such a necessary fixture in his life. He couldn't imagine her going back to Barcelona. He wanted her here by his side, holding his hand just as she was now.

"Serafia?" he asked, his voice quiet and serious.

"Yes?"

"Would you...consider staying here in Alma? With me?"

She turned to him and studied his face with her dark eyes. "You're going to be fine, Gabriel. You've improved so much. You're not going to need my help any longer."

Gabriel rolled onto his side. "I don't want you here for your help. I'm not interested in you being my employee, I want you to be my girlfriend."

Her eyes grew wide as he spoke, her teeth drawing in her bottom lip while she considered his offer. Not exactly the enthusiastic response he was hoping for.

"You don't want to stay," he noted.

Serafia sat up, pulling her hand away from

his to wrap her arms around her knees. "I do and I don't. I have a life in Barcelona, Gabriel. A quiet, easy life that I love. Giving that up to come here and be with you is a big decision. Being the king's girlfriend is no quiet, easy life. I don't know if I'm ready."

Gabriel sat up beside her and put a comforting hand on her shoulder. He knew he was asking a lot of her, but he couldn't bear the idea of living in Alma without her. "You don't have to decide right now. Just think on it."

She looked at him with relief in her eyes. "Okay, I will."

After a day at sea, they'd returned to the house and taken naps. They decided to dine al fresco on the patio outside his bedroom. It was just sunset as they reconvened with glasses of wine to watch the sun sink into the sea. The sky was an amazing mix of purples, oranges and reds, all overtaken by inky blackness as the night finally fell upon Alma.

It was beautifully peaceful, but Serafia felt

anything but. Despite the surroundings, the wine and the company, she couldn't get Gabriel's offer out of her mind. To stay in Alma, to be his girlfriend publically…that would change her entire life. She wasn't sure she was ready for that, even though her feelings for him grew every day.

The king didn't have a girlfriend. At least not for long. Unless something went wrong pretty quickly, being his girlfriend would mean soon being his fiancée, and then his queen. That meant she would never return home to her quiet life in Barcelona.

But was that life becoming too quiet? Had she been hiding there instead of living?

The questions still plagued her as they finished the last of the roasted chicken Marta had made for dinner. She felt pleasantly full as she eased back in her chair, a sensation she wasn't used to. She might be comfortable hiding from the world in her hacienda, but she wasn't living her life and she wasn't really getting better. She was managing her disease, controlling it almost to the point that she'd once let it control her. But in Alma, with Gabriel, the dark thoughts hadn't once crept into her mind. He was good for her. And she was good for him.

Maybe coming here was the right choice. Her heart certainly wanted to stay.

She didn't have to decide now, she reflected, and the thought soothed her nerves. To distract herself, she decided now was the right time to give Gabriel his gift. "I got you something."

Gabriel looked at her in surprise and set down his glass of wine. "Really? You didn't have to do that."

"I know. But I did it, anyway." Serafia got up and went to her room, returning a moment later with a small black box.

Gabriel accepted it and flipped open the hinged lid. She watched his face light up as he saw what was inside. "Wow!" He scooped the gift out of the box, setting it aside so he could admire his gift with both hands. "A pocket watch! That's great. Thank you."

Gabriel leaned in to give her a thank-you

kiss before returning to admiring his gift. The pocket watch was a Patek Philippe, crafted with eighteen-karat yellow gold. It cost more than a nice BMW, but Serafia didn't care. She wanted to buy him something nice that she knew he didn't have. "I told you in Miami that I would find a way to get around your watch issue."

"And you've done a splendid job. It's beautiful."

"It comes with a chain so you can attach it inside your suit coat."

He nodded, running his fingertip along the shiny curve of the glass. Closing the box, he put it on the table and stood up. He approached her slowly, wrapping his arms around her waist and tugging her tight against him. "Thank you. That was an amazingly thoughtful gift."

Serafia smiled, pleased that he liked it. When she bought it, she wasn't sure if he would see it as a further criticism of his time-management issues or if he would feel it was too old-fashioned for him. She'd known it was perfect the moment she saw it, and she was pleased to finally know that he agreed.

"I feel like I need to get you something now," he said.

"Not at all," she insisted. "After our discussions about watches earlier and realizing why you disliked them so much, I knew this was something I wanted to do for you. There's no need to reciprocate."

He stared at her lips as she spoke, but shook his head ever so slightly when she was finished. "I'll do what I like," he insisted. "If that means buying you something beautiful and sparkly, I will. If that means taking you into that bedroom and making love to you until you're hoarse, I will."

"Sounds like a challenge," she said.

When his lips met hers, the worries in her mind faded away. Serafia wrapped her arms around his neck and melted into him. The roar of the waves below was the only sound except for the pounding of her heart.

After a moment, he started backing them into

the bedroom. Their lips were still pressed together as they moved across the tile to the king-size bed against the far wall. Serafia clung to him, losing herself in touching and tasting Gabriel. No matter what happened each day, she knew it was okay because she knew he would help her forget all her worries each night.

When her calves met with the bed, they stopped. Serafia tugged at his shirt, pulling it up and over his head. She ran her fingertips across his bare chest and scattered soft kisses along his collarbone. His skin was warm from a day in the sun and scented with the handmade soaps they kept in the bathrooms here.

She felt Gabriel's fingertips on her outer thighs, slowly gathering up the fabric of her dress. Before he could pull it any higher, she turned them around so that his back was to the bed. Then she shoved, thrusting him onto the mattress, where he sprawled out and bounced.

"Are we playing rough tonight?" he asked with a laugh.

Serafia shook her head and took a few steps

backward. "I just wanted you to sit back and enjoy the view."

Pushing aside her self-consciousness, she let the straps of her sundress fall from her shoulders, the soft cotton dress pooling at her feet. She coyly turned her back to him, unfastening her bra and letting it drop to the floor. With a sly glance over her shoulder at him, she slipped her thumbs beneath her cheeky lace panties and slid them down her legs. Completely nude, she turned back to face him.

Gabriel watched from the bed with a glint of appreciation in his eyes. He really, truly thought she was beautiful, and knowing this made her feel beautiful. She lifted her arms to brush the cascading waves of her hair over her shoulders, displaying her breasts and narrow waist. He swallowed hard as he watched her, his jaw tightening.

"Come here," he said.

Serafia took her time, despite his royal command. She sauntered over to the bed, crawling across the coverlet on all fours until she was hovering between his thighs. She reached for the fly of his jeans, but the moment she was within Gabriel's reach, he lunged for her. Before she knew quite what had happened, she was on her back and the weight of Gabriel's body was pressing her into the soft mattress.

He kissed her, his mouth hard and demanding against her own. His fingertips pressed into her, just as hard. She gasped for air when he pulled away to taste her throat. His teeth grazed her delicate skin, almost as though he wanted to mark her, claim her as his own.

She wanted to be his. His alone. At least for tonight. She could feel his desire against her bare thigh, the rough denim keeping them apart. She reached between them, slipping her hand beneath his waistband to grip the length of him. He growled against her throat, leaning into her for a moment, and then reluctantly pulling away before she wore out the last of his self-control.

Slipping off the edge of the bed, he removed the last of his clothes, sheathed himself in latex and returned to his home between her thighs.

Without saying a word, he drove into her, stretching her body to its limit. She cried out and clung to his back, her fingernails pressing crescents into his skin.

Their lovemaking was more frantic tonight, more passionate and intense. She wasn't sure if it was the end of their relationship looming that pushed them to a frenzy, but she happily went along for the ride. Nothing else mattered as he drove into her again and again. All she could do was give in to the pleasure, live in the moment and not let the future intrude on their night together. It wasn't hard. Within minutes he had her gasping and on the verge of unraveling.

That was when he stopped moving entirely.

Her eyes flew open, her breath ragged. "Is something wrong?" she asked.

"Stay with me," he demanded.

She wanted to. She wanted to give him her body, her heart and her soul. In that moment, she knew she already had. Despite her hesitation, despite her worries, she had fallen in love with Gabriel Montoro, future king of Alma. But was she good for him? Would she be the queen the country needed?

Those critical articles were just the first of many she was sure would surface. Rumors about her family wouldn't disappear overnight. She didn't want to bring scandal to the new monarchy. It was too new, too fragile. She couldn't risk that, even for love.

She also couldn't risk herself. Would she slip back into her old habits with the eyes of an entire country on her? It was a dangerous prospect.

But when he looked at her like that, his green eyes pleading with her, how could she say no? She wanted to stay. She wanted to be with him, to help him on his new journey. If that meant she might someday be queen and take on all the pressures and joys that entailed…so be it.

"Yes," she whispered into the darkness before she could change her mind.

Gabriel thrust hard into her and she was lost. The waves of emotions and pleasure collided inside her, making her cry out desperately. She repeated her answer again and again, encouraging him and confirming to herself that she truly meant it. She loved him and she was going to stay.

His release came quickly after hers. He groaned loud against her throat, surging into her one last time as he came undone. Serafia held him, cradling his hips between her thighs until it was over.

When he'd finally stilled, she heard him whisper almost undetectably in her ear, "Thank you."

He was grateful that she'd agreed to stay. She just hoped that would still be the case in the upcoming weeks.

Ten

Serafia should've woken up on cloud nine. She was in love, she'd agreed to stay in Alma with Gabriel and everything was perfect. And yet there was a cloud hanging over her head. It was as though she couldn't let herself breathe, couldn't let herself believe that this was really going to work between them, until after today.

Today was the last hurdle before the coronation. After today's public appearance, Gabriel would have met all the initial requirements and could settle quietly into his life at Alma while the preparation for the coronation took place. She didn't anticipate any problems today. All they had to do was make it through the tour of one of Patrick Rowling's oil platforms off the coast, but for some reason, she woke up anxious.

They got on the road after breakfast, driving the hour back into Del Sol, where they would take a helicopter out to sea. Helicopters. Better safe than sorry, she decided to get his opinion on it during their drive to the capital.

"Are you okay with helicopters?" Serafia asked.

Gabriel straightened his tie and nodded. "Helicopters are fine. The weather seems pretty calm today, so it shouldn't be a bumpy ride."

"Good." She sighed with relief. That was one less worry. "The only other option to get out there is to take a boat and get lifted by crane onto the platform while you cling to a rope and metal cage called a Billy Pugh. I wasn't looking forward to that at all."

Gabriel smiled. "That actually sounds pretty cool."

"You're the rebellious one," she said. "I'm interested in staying alive."

"Fair enough. How far out is the oil platform?"

Serafia looked down at her tablet as their car approached the heliport. "The one we're going to is about twelve kilometers off the coast. It's the newest one they've constructed and Patrick is very eager to show off his new toy."

Gabriel frowned. "I'm sure he is."

"What's that face about?"

"I'm not sure how I feel about the Rowlings yet. At least Patrick. He seems a little showy, a little too cocky for my taste. His sons seem nice enough, although I can't wait to see the look on Bella's face when she's introduced to the guy Dad wants her to marry. If there aren't instant fireworks between them, she just might kill our father in his sleep. We might need her to stay at the beach house when she gets here."

"I wouldn't worry too much about Patrick or Bella today. I'm sure the trip will be fine and you'll be off the hook for a while until the coronation. Today, we'll be flying over with Prime Minister Rivera. He asked to join us on the tour."

"What about Hector?"

"Apparently he doesn't do helicopters, but he's briefed everyone and he'll be meeting with you afterward to go over how it went with Rivera."

"That's fine. I've only had one short meeting with the prime minister, so it's probably a good idea to have some more face time. I don't think we'll get much talking done in the helicopter, though. Aren't they loud?"

Serafia had never been in one, but she'd heard they were. "Yes. I'm pretty sure you won't be conducting any business in the helicopter."

He nodded and relaxed back into the seat. "Good. I'm not sure I'm ready for any hard-core discussions. Is the helicopter large enough for the royal guard, as well? That's quite a few of us to fit into one."

Serafia shook her head. "They've already got a crew of guards there at the rig. They cleared the platform this morning and are standing by for your arrival. All the details have been taken care of," she assured him. Turning to glance out the window, she realized they were at their destination. "And here we are."

They climbed from the car at the heliport and made their way over to the helicopter waiting for them. The prime minister was already there, rushing over to shake Gabriel's hand. Then as a group, they climbed into the helicopter and headed out to sea.

Serafia was glad Gabriel was okay with helicopters. She wasn't exactly thrilled with the idea, so it was good that at least one of them wasn't freaking out. When the engine started, she put on the ear protection and closed her eyes. The liftoff sent her stomach into her throat, but after a few minutes the movement was steady. Thankfully it wouldn't take long to get out there, so she took some deep breaths and tried not to think about where she was.

A thump startled her, and she opened her eyes in panic only to realize they'd already landed on the oil platform. Thank goodness. Everyone climbed out and Patrick came to greet them. With him, he had the lead rig operator, his son

William and a few members of Patrick's management team who always seemed to be following him around. This, in addition to a large contingent of press, as always. They'd come out earlier on the boat. Once everyone was fitted with hard hats, the tour began.

With all the cameras so near today, Serafia decided to take a step back from Gabriel. There was no need to stir any more rumors or give any of them a reason to write another scathing article about her family or their romance. He didn't seem to notice she was gone. With everything going on, he surged ahead, carried by the crowd with Rivera and Patrick Rowling at his side.

Serafia trailed the group as they walked around the open decks of the platform, admiring the massive drill and other equipment. She couldn't hear what Patrick and the others were saying, but she didn't mind. She wasn't really that interested.

After that, they went inside to tour the employee quarters and cafeteria, the offices and the control room. It was a tight fit for the men who lived on the rig up to two weeks at a stretch.

The day was going fairly well, so far. She'd begun to think she'd been anxious for no reason.

It wasn't until they went back outside and started climbing down a set of metal stairs that went below the platform that Serafia started to feel the niggling of worry in the back of her mind. The only thing below the platform were the emergency evacuation boats, some maintenance equipment and the underwater exploration pod they used for maintenance.

Oh God. Her heart very nearly leaped out of her chest and into her throat when she realized what was about to happen.

The submarine.

She'd forgotten all about it. It had always been a part of the plan. They were to tour the oil rig, and then their exploration pod, which was essentially a small, four-man submarine, would take Gabriel under the surface to see the rig at work. It was a harmless photo op, and when she was given the original itinerary, she hadn't thought a thing about it. Gabriel certainly hadn't mentioned having a problem with it when they discussed the agenda back in Miami.

Since then, she'd learned about Gabriel's issues with small, dark spaces, but so much had happened that the submarine had slipped her mind.

That had to be where they were going. Unfortunately there were twenty people between Gabriel and her on the narrow deck and staircase. He was below the platform and she was stuck above it at the very back of the pack. She was unable to get close enough to warn him before it was too late.

She rushed to the metal railing, peering over the side at the party below. They were still walking around while Patrick pointed out one thing or another, but she could see the open hatch of the exploration pod a few yards in front of them.

"Gabriel!" she shouted, but no one but a few of the reporters and crew members turned to look at her. The sounds of the ocean and the operating rig easily drowned out everything. Everything but the expression on his face.

Serafia knew the instant that he realized where they were going. He stiffened, his jaw tightening. His hands curled into fists at his side. Everyone around him continued to talk and laugh, but he wasn't participating in the discussion. He was loosening his tie, looking around for another option to escape, short of leaping into the ocean and swimming back to the mainland.

Patrick Rowling and the prime minister were the first to crawl inside the exploration pod. Gabriel stood there at the entrance for several moments, looking into the small space. He was white as a sheet and he gripped the railing with white-knuckled intensity. She could tell the others were trying to encourage him, but he likely couldn't hear anything they said if he was having a full-blown panic attack.

Then he shook his head. Backing up, he nearly ran into someone else, then turned and pushed his way through the crowd back to the stairs. Serafia could barely make out the sounds of shouts and words of concern. Patrick climbed back out of the submarine, calling toward Gabriel, but he didn't stop. He leaped up the stairs, finally colliding with Serafia as he reached the top.

He looked at her, but his eyes were wild with panic. It seemed almost as if he didn't really see her at all.

"I'm so sorry, Gabriel. I forgot all about the submarine. I would've warned you if I remembered."

He looked at her, his expression hardening. There was venom in his gaze, a place where she'd only ever seen attraction and humor. She reached out for his arm, but he shoved it aside and took a step back.

"It's not a big deal," she reassured him. "They can go on ahead without you. I'm sure you're not the only person who doesn't fancy the idea of a ride in that thing."

The look on his face made it clear that he didn't agree. It was a big deal, at least to him.

Without saying a word, he turned and took off down the metal-grated walkway toward the helipad.

"Gabriel, stop! Wait!" she shouted as she pursued him, but he kept on going. She finally gave up just as she was overtaken by the press. They pushed her aside as they chased Gabriel, but before they could reach him, she spied the helicopter rising over the top of the rig.

With nothing else she could do, Serafia stood and watched the helicopter disappear into the horizon. Once it was gone, all she could see, all she could think of, was the look of utter betrayal on his face. He blamed her for this. And maybe he should. She'd made a very big error today.

"What happened?" The prime minister stopped beside her, his brow pinched in confusion. "Is the prince okay? He looked quite ill."

"I don't know," Serafia said. She wasn't going to be the one to tell him, and any of the surrounding reporters, that Gabriel was claustrophobic. That would make it seem as if she was deliberately trying to undermine him. He should've been the one to say it. All it would've taken was a polite pass and he could've avoided it. Instead, he'd run like he'd been ambushed.

A sinking feeling settled into Serafia's stomach at the thought. Was that what Gabriel believed she was doing? This was just one oversight, but when added to the string of other problems they'd had over the last week, did it add up to the appearance of sabotage? He couldn't possibly believe she'd do that to him. He hadn't given that newspaper article a second thought.

Or had he?

Serafia feared he'd begun to suspect her. That look had said everything. Serafia had ruined it. She hadn't meant to, but she'd ruined her relationship with Gabriel before it ever started.

Even though Gabriel had his driver take him back to Playa del Onda right away, he was discouraged to find Hector already waiting for him there. Judging by his press secretary's dour expression, the news of the incident on the oil rig had beaten Gabriel home. He just wanted to take off his tie, pour a glass of scotch and relax, but Hector was the hitch in that plan.

"Where's Serafia?" he asked as Gabriel blew past him.

"I don't know. I left her at the oil platform."

Hector made a thoughtful noise and followed him into the den. Gabriel poured a drink and ripped off his tie before collapsing onto the couch. "Why?"

"Well, I wanted to speak to you privately about those rumors. I'm concerned that the Espinas may be trying to undermine your coronation."

Gabriel was tired of hearing about this. "We've discussed this already."

"Yes, but that was before the prime minister called and briefed me about what happened today. He was concerned about you. He'd heard about the incident at the winery, as well."

Great. Now they were talking about him and his issues behind his back. "I don't do well in small spaces," Gabriel explained. "When I start having a panic attack, I have a very aggressive flight response. I overreact, I'm aware of that, but in the moment, I just have to get away from the situation. All the pressure I'm under to be poised and perfect every moment is just making it that much worse because I try to fight my way through it and it doesn't work. Then I feel like a fool."

Hector listened carefully. "I'll make certain we don't have these issues in the future. In exchange, I ask that you speak up when you're uncomfortable so we don't make a bigger scene out of it. Does Serafia know about your claustrophobia?"

"Yes." She didn't know until after the winery incident, but she knew today.

"I see. Your Majesty, my concern is about why these situations keep popping up. Rivera said he asked Patrick Rowling about the submarine and said that it had been Serafia's idea. I understand that you two are…whatever you are. But you really need to put your feelings for her aside and consider the possibility that all these

unfortunate incidents are actually carefully orchestrated by the Espina family."

Gabriel dropped his face into his hand. He'd
had a horrible day and he didn't really want to
face this right now. "I'll take care of it," he said.

"Your Majesty, I—"

"I said, I'll take care of it!" Gabriel shouted.
Suddenly his overwhelming apprehension had
morphed into anger. He knew he shouldn't direct it at Hector, but he didn't care. He would
kill the messenger because he didn't know what
else to do.

"Very good, Your Grace. Thank you for your
time." Hector gave a curt bow and left the room.

Gabriel watched Hector leave, the questions
and anxiety spinning in his mind. Unable to
sit still, he headed out to the veranda to await
Serafia's return to the compound. The longer
he waited, the more his blood began to heat in
his veins. He had been upset at the oil platform,
but after his discussion with Hector, every minute that ticked by tipped his emotions over into
pure anger.

If he was right, this was the ultimate betrayal. Serafia would've known exactly what she was doing. She knew he couldn't stand small, confined spaces. How could she schedule him for what amounted to a miniature submarine ride under an oil platform? Even people who hadn't been through the kind of experience he'd had would balk at that. And yet, he felt this pressure as the future king to do it. He had to be strong; he couldn't show weakness. His father expected it. His country expected it. And all it did was backfire on him and make him look like more of a coward when he fled.

The situation had snuck up on him. They were walking around the lower level and the next thing he knew, he was confronted with his personal nightmare. As he'd looked down into the small round hatch at the metal ladder that would take him into a space too cramped for more than four full-grown men, he felt himself launch into a full-blown panic attack.

This wasn't like the incident at the vineyard. There, the room was dark and underground, but he could escape any time he chose, and did. The minute Gabriel climbed down that ladder, and the hatch was sealed, he would be trapped. His lungs had seized up as if a vise was crushing his rib cage. His heart had been racing so quickly he could barely tell the rhythm of one beat from the next. He'd been sweating, wheezing and damn near on the verge of crying while Patrick Rowling and the prime minister tried to coax him on board.

No way. He didn't care if he offended the richest man in Alma. He wasn't about to have that image on him on television, blasted around the internet and on the front page of every paper. New King of Alma Cries Like a Baby When Forced Into a Submarine! They might as well send a stamped invitation for the Tantaberra family to come back and take over again. It was better to leave before it got worse.

It was bad enough everyone had witnessed his behavior. The Rowlings, the press and even the prime minister were all standing by as he'd completely flipped out, shoved people aside to escape and run across the platform to the helicopter pad as if he were on fire. It must have been a sight to see…his guards chasing after him, people shouting at him to come back, the press recording every moment of it… *The Runaway King*. Now, there was a nickname for his upcoming illustrious reign.

He hadn't registered much in the moment. Gabriel had only been motivated by a driving need to get away from that submarine, off the platform and onto dry land with sunshine on his face as soon as possible. But he could hear Serafia as she'd tried to comfort him. He'd registered the panic and worry on her face as she rushed toward him, but he wasn't slowing down for her or anyone else. Besides, it had been too late. The damage was already done.

Of course, that might have been part of her plan, right? The article had insinuated that the Espina family was determined to gain the throne back one way or another. If not through seduction, perhaps through scandal and humiliation. Serafia had been throwing grenades at him since he arrived. The watch, the debacle at the airport, the vineyard and now the oil platform… Even the supposedly successful party at Rowling's house had proven controversial when he snubbed the Gomez girl at Serafia's suggestion.

He'd paid her to help this week go smoothly, to prepare him for any eventuality as king, and it had started to seem more as if she was deliberately setting him up to fail.

He heard the sound of his bedroom door open. After taking a large sip of his scotch, he set the mostly empty glass down. The amber liquid burned in his stomach, just as his anger shot hot through his veins.

Finally Serafia stepped through the open doorway, looking as worn and ragged as if she'd jogged all the way back from the oil platform. Her shirt was untucked and wrinkled. There was a run in her stocking, and her heels were scuffed. Her hair had been up in a bun, but now it was half up, half down in a silky black mess. She was flushed, with bloodshot eyes and dried tear tracks down her cheeks. It made him wonder how long it had taken her to put together this look and assume the role of the innocent in all this. Maybe that was why it took forever for her to get here.

"I'm so sorry, Gabriel. I didn't—"

"Just stop!" he shouted more forcefully than he intended. The anger that had simmered inside him was approaching a full boil now that he was face-to-face with her again. "Don't tell me you didn't know about this, because I know that's a lie." He gestured to the white sheet of paper on the table in front of him. "I found the schedule you gave me back in Miami for this week. This event was on there. Patrick Rowling said you actually suggested it. You knew all this time what we were building up to."

Serafia crossed her arms over her chest in a defensive posture. "In Miami, I didn't know anything about your abduction. Yes, it was my suggestion because I thought it would be an interesting activity for you. When we reviewed your schedule for the visit, I mentioned it and you said nothing. You just tuned me out half the time. I'm surprised you even had the schedule anymore."

"And after you knew about what happened to me in Venezuela? After the incident at the vineyard? Did it not occur to you then that these plans for the visit to the oil platform might be a bad idea?"

"I'd forgotten," she said, tears forming in her eyes again. "With everything that has happened over the past week, I forgot all about the submarine. It slipped my mind and by the time I remembered, it was too late. We were separated by the crowd and I couldn't warn you without making a scene. I was trying to warn you before they got to that part of the tour."

Gabriel stood up, his dark gaze searching her face for signs of the treachery he knew was there. Hector had helped him cast her under a shadow of suspicion he couldn't shake. She'd been hiding her secret agenda beneath a disguise of coy smiles and stiff, respectable suits, but it was there nonetheless. And he'd fallen for it.

"And you showed up to warn me at the perfect time," he replied with bitterness in his voice. "Late enough for me to embarrass myself and undermine my future as king, but not so late as to convince me that it was deliberate just in case the ploy didn't work and you might still end up queen."

A strange combination of emotions danced across Serafia's face, ending in a look of exasperation. "I don't want to be queen. I never have and you know why!"

If she really didn't want to be queen, that only left one option. "Just wanting to stay close enough to ruin me and my family, then?"

Serafia threw her arms up, spinning in a circle before facing him with her index finger held up. "One incident. *One*. And suddenly those newspaper accusations you dismissed are gospel? Do you have no faith in me at all?"

"I did. For some stupid reason, I pushed aside all my suspicions and allowed myself to trust you more than I've trusted anyone in years. Even when that article came out, I dismissed it as nasty gossip or old news from another time and place. I couldn't believe that you could be using me to get to the throne."

"Because I'm not," she insisted.

Gabriel just shook his head sadly. "You're just as bad as the Gomez family. You know what? You're even worse. At least they're transparent about their ambitions. You and your family just sidle up to us like friends, then pervert the entire relationship to suit your own purposes."

"Gabriel, you said yourself that that story was nonsense. I didn't get planted with you. You hired me."

That was the detail that had bothered him, but the longer he sat on the patio, the more he'd begun to wonder if that was really true. "What *were* you doing in Miami, Serafia? I hadn't seen you in years, and then all of a sudden, you fly all the way to Miami from Barcelona for my going-away party? You could've just waited to see me in Alma if you were that interested in congratulating me, and saved yourself a fortune in time and money."

Serafia stiffened, her eyebrows drawing together into a frown. "I was in the States for another project and my father asked me to attend on behalf of the family."

"What project?" he pressed. "Who were you working for?"

Serafia started to stutter over her words, as though she was failing to come up with an adequate lie when she was put on the spot. "I—it w-was for a confidential client. I can't tell you who it was."

"A confidential client? Of course it was." Gabriel tried not to take it personally that she thought he was so stupid. "You may not have been a plant, but you were a tempting little worm dangling on a hook right in front of me. I snatched you up just as surely as you'd weaseled your way into my inner circle on your own. You pretended to help me be a better king, building up my confidence in and out of bed,

while slowly undermining every inch of progress I've made along the way."

Serafia looked at him with hurt reflecting in
her dark eyes. "Is that all you think of the two
of us? Of what we have together?"

"I didn't at first, but now I see how wrong I
was. I can see it must have been really difficult
for you."

She narrowed her gaze at him, her tears fad-
ing. "What must be?"

Gabriel swallowed hard and spat out the words
he'd been holding in all day. "Trying to screw
me in two different ways at once."

Serafia gasped and raised her hand to cover
her mouth. She stumbled back on her heels until
her back collided with the doorframe. "You're
a bastard, Gabriel."

"Maybe," he said thoughtfully. "But it's people like you who made me this way."

"I quit!" she shouted, disappearing into the
house.

"Fine. Quit!" he yelled back at her. "I was just
going to fire you, anyway."

He heard her bedroom door slam shut down the hallway. With her gone, the anger that had boiled over suddenly drained out of him. He slumped back into his chair and dropped his head into his hands.

It didn't matter whether she quit or he fired her. In the end, the damage was done and she would soon be gone.

Eleven

Harder. Faster. Keep pushing.

It didn't matter if Serafia's lungs were burning or that her leg muscles felt as if they could rip from her bones at any second. She had to keep going.

Just when she hit the point where she couldn't take any more, she reached out for the console and dropped the speed on the treadmill by half a mile. Giving herself only a minute or two to recover, she then increased it by a whole mile. Her sneakers pounded hard against the rotating belt, which was reaching speeds she could barely maintain in the past.

But she had to now. She had to keep running or everything would catch up with her. It wasn't until she could feel her heart pounding like Thor's hammer against her breast that she realized she'd taken this too far. She reached out and pounded the emergency stop button, slamming into the console and draping her broken body over it. The air rushing from her lungs blazed like fire, her heart feeling as if it was about to burst. She'd run for miles today. Hours. Longer and harder than her doctor-appointed forty-five-minute daily limit.

And yet the moment she looked up, the world around her was just the same. The same heartache. The same confusion. The same anger at herself and at Gabriel. All she'd managed to do was pull a hamstring and sweat through her clothes.

She gripped her bottle of water and stepped down onto the tile floor with gelatinous, quivering legs. Unable to go much farther, she opened the door to her garden courtyard. The cold water and ocean breeze weren't enough to soothe her overheated body, so she set down her bottle and approached her swimming pool. Without stopping to take off her shoes, she stepped off the edge, plunging herself into the cool turquoise depths.

Rising to the surface, she pushed her hair out of her face and took a deep breath. She felt a million times better. Her heart slowed and her body temperature was jerked back from the point of disaster.

And yet she was still at a loss over what to do with herself. She had returned home to Barcelona in disgrace. Her last-minute flight had delivered her home late in the night; she hadn't even told her family or staff that she was returning. All she knew was that she had to get out of Alma that instant. She would work the rest out later.

Once she'd escaped…she didn't know what to do. She had no jobs lined up for several weeks. She'd cleared her calendar when she took the Montoro job because she wasn't sure how long it would truly take. The first few days in Miami had been excruciating and she'd wondered if two weeks would be enough.

Two weeks were more than enough, at least for her. And while she was relieved to be home, returned to the sanctuary she'd built for herself here, something felt off. She'd wandered through the empty halls, sat on the balcony overlooking the sea, lay in bed staring at the ceiling…the thought of Gabriel crept into everything she did.

Serafia swam to the edge of the pool and crossed her arms along the stone, lifting her torso up out of the water. She dropped her head onto her forearms and fought the tears that had taunted her the last few days. As hard as she'd resisted falling for the rebellious prince, it had happened, anyway. Even with the threat of returning to the spotlight, the potential for becoming queen and all the responsibilities that held, she couldn't help herself.

And then he turned on her. How could he think she would do something like that on purpose? The minute she realized where they were headed, the panic had been nearly overwhelming. And then when he'd looked at her with the betrayal reflecting in his eyes, she felt her heart break. He was so used to people using and abusing his trust that he refused to see that wasn't what she was doing.

Perhaps she should have stayed in Alma and fought to clear her name. Running away made her look guilty, but she just couldn't stay there. Her family might have been from Alma decades ago, but she was born and raised in Spain and that was where she needed to be.

She just needed to get her life back on track. The dramas of Alma would fade, Gabriel would choose his queen and she would go on with her life, such as it was.

At least that was what she told herself.

The French doors to the courtyard opened behind her, and Serafia's housekeeper stepped out with a tray. "I have your lunch ready, señorita."

Serafia swam back to the shallow end of the pool to greet her. She wasn't remotely interested in food with the way she felt, but it would hurt her housekeeper's feelings if she didn't pretend otherwise. "Thank you, Esperanza. Please leave it on the patio table."

Esperanza did as she asked, hesitating a moment by the edge of the pool with a towel in her hands. She seemed worried, her wrinkled face pinched into an expression of concern. "Are you going to eat it?"

Serafia frowned and climbed up the steps. "What do you mean?"

"You barely touched your breakfast, just picking at the fruit. I found most of last night's dinner plate scraped into the trash so I wouldn't see it. I have all your favorite snacks and drinks in the house since your return and I haven't had to restock a single thing."

Serafia snatched the towel from the housekeeper's hands, the past anxiety of being caught in the act rushing back to her. "That's none of your business. I pay you to cook my meals, not monitor them like my mother."

The hurt expression on the older woman's face made her feel instantly guilty for snapping at her. Esperanza was the sweetest woman she knew and she didn't deserve that kind of treatment. "I'm sorry. I shouldn't have said that. Forgive me." Serafia slipped down into the patio chair and buried her face in her towel.

"It's nothing. When I don't eat, I get grumpy, too," Esperanza offered with a small smile. She was a plump older woman with a perpetually pleasant disposition. Probably because she got to eat and wasn't eternally stressing out about how she looked. "But I worry about you, señorita, and so do your parents."

Serafia's head snapped up. "They've called?"

"*Sí*, but you were out walking on the beach. They asked me not to tell you. They seemed very interested in your eating habits, which is why I noticed the change. They said if you started visibly losing weight, I should call them straightaway."

Great. Her parents were having her own employee spy on her. They must really be concerned. Serafia sighed and sat back in her chair. They probably were right to be. In the last few days since returning from Alma, she'd already lost five pounds that she shouldn't have. She was at the low end of the range her doctors had provided her. If she got back into the red zone, she risked another round of inpatient treatment, and she didn't want to do that.

Damn it.

"Thank you for caring about me, Esperanza." Serafia eyed the tray of food she brought her. There was a large green salad with diced chicken, a platter with a hard-boiled egg, slices of cheese and bread and a carafe of vinaigrette. Ever hopeful, Esperanza had even included two of her famous cinnamon-sugar cookies. All in all, it was a healthy, balanced lunch with plenty of vegetables, proteins and whole grains. The kind Serafia asked her to make most days.

And yet she had a hard time stopping her brain from mentally obsessing over how many calories were sitting there. If she only ate the greens and the chicken with no dressing, it wouldn't be too bad. Maybe one piece of cheese, but definitely no bread. They were the same compulsive thoughts that she'd once allowed to take over her life. She'd battled this demon for a long time. A part of her had hoped that she'd beaten it for good, but one emotional blow had sent her spiraling back into her old bad habits.

Habits that had almost killed her.

"It looks wonderful," she said. "I promise to eat every bite. Are there any more cookies?"

"There are!" Esperanza said, her face brightening.

"I'll take some of those this afternoon after my siesta."

"Muy bien!" Esperanza shuffled back into the house, leaving Serafia alone on the patio.

She knew she should change out of her wet workout clothes, but she didn't care. She knew that she needed to eat. Now. Voices in her head be damned.

She started with one of the cookies for good measure. It dropped into her empty stomach like lead, reminding her to take it slow. Her doctors had warned her about starving herself, then binging. That was another, all new, dangerous path she was determined not to take.

Nibbling on the cheese and bread, she started to feel better. She knew that her body paid a high toll for her anorexia. As she was driven to exercise and ignore all the food she could, it made her feel terrible. Even this small amount of food made the difference. Picking up her fork and pouring some of the vinaigrette over the salad, she speared a bite and chewed it thoughtfully.

All this was in marked contrast to the way she'd felt in Alma. For some reason, her past worries had slipped away as she focused on preparing Gabriel to be king. Perhaps it was because he thought she was so beautiful, even with the extra pounds she resented. He worshipped every inch of her body in bed, never once stopping to criticize or comment on her flaws. That made her feel beautiful. When they ate together, it was a fun, enjoyable experience. She was too distracted by the good food and even better company to worry about the calories. There were a few days in Alma where she'd even forgotten to exercise. Before that, she hadn't missed a day of exercise in years. When she was with Gabriel, she'd been able to stop fighting with her disease and simply *live*.

She had been doing so well, and the minute it was yanked away from her, the negative thoughts came rushing back in. She couldn't do this. If there was one thing she'd learned in the years since her heart attack, it was that she loved herself too much to keep hurting herself.

Reaching for a slice of bread with cheese, she took a large bite, then another, and another, until her lunch was very nearly gone.

She couldn't allow loving Gabriel to undo all the progress she'd made.

The report on Gabriel's lap told him what he already knew in his heart, but somehow, seeing the words in black-and-white made him feel that much more like the ass he was.

Hector had done as he'd asked. His people in the press office had reached out to the author of the scathing article on the Espinas. It hadn't taken much pressure for him to reveal that he'd been approached by Felicia Gomez. He admitted that while the historical portions of the article were researched and fact-checked, the insinuations of Serafia's nefarious intentions were purely speculation based on Felicia's suggestions. It didn't mean that her family didn't help overthrow the Montoros, but in the end, that really didn't matter anymore. All that mattered was that Serafia was innocent of all those charges.

He knew it. He knew it when he'd read the article the first time and he knew it when he'd thrown accusations at Serafia and watched her heart break right before his eyes. He'd been humiliated. Angry. He'd lashed out at her because he'd allowed his own fears to rule his life and publically embarrass him. It was easier to blame her in the moment than face the fact that he'd done this to himself.

Gabriel felt awful about the whole thing. Serafia had been the only person in his life he thought he could trust, and yet he'd turned around and abused her trust of him at the first provocation. It made him feel sick.

He needed to do something to fix this. Right now.

Looking up from his report, he spied Luca walking down the hallway past his office. "Luca, can you find out if the Montoro jet is still in Alma?"

Luca nodded and disappeared down the hallway.

Gabriel took a deep breath and resolved himself to his sudden decision. He didn't entirely have his plan together, but he knew he needed to get out of Alma to make this happen. That meant getting on a plane. Serafia had returned to Barcelona. He was certain she wouldn't answer his calls if he tried, and anyway, he knew in his heart that they needed to have a conversation in person. The only catch would be whether or not the jet was here. His father had sent for Bella to come to Alma. Gabriel wasn't sure what day that was happening, but if the jet was with her in Miami, he'd have to find another way to get to Serafia. Could a prince fly coach?

He didn't care if he was crammed in a middle seat at the back of the plane, he had to get to her. Saying he was sorry wasn't enough. He needed to follow that up with how he felt about her. It had taken losing her for him to get in touch with how he truly felt. There was nothing quite like waking up and realizing he was in love and he'd just ruined everything.

But maybe, just maybe, apologizing and confessing his love for her would be enough for Serafia to forgive his snap judgments.

Luca appeared in the doorway, an odd expression on his face.

"Where's the jet?" Gabriel asked.

"It's still at the airport in Del Sol, Your Grace."

He breathed a sigh of relief. "Good. Tell them I want to go to Barcelona as soon as possible. I need a car to meet me at the airport and I need someone to track down Serafia's home address. I have no idea where she lives."

"Yes, Your Grace. I will see to all that. But first, you have…a visitor."

Gabriel could feel his own face taking on Luca's pinched, confused expression. "A visitor?" Could people just stroll up to the royal beach compound and knock on the door to join him for tea?

"Yes. It's an old woman from Del Sol. She told the guards at the gate that she took a taxi out here to speak with you. She said it's very important."

Gabriel was certain that everything people wanted to say to the king was very important, but he was at a loss. He wanted to pack his bag and be in Barcelona before dinnertime. Certainly this could wait…

"She says it's about Serafia."

Gabriel stiffened. That changed everything. "Have her escorted into the parlor. Tell Marta to bring some tea and those almond cookies if we have any left. That will give us some time to make the arrangements before I leave."

Luca nodded and went off to fulfill his

wishes. Gabriel returned to his closet to pick a suit coat. He'd been dressing himself for the last few days and if he was honest with himself, he wasn't doing a very good job. He knew that Serafia would want him to wear a jacket to greet a guest, especially an elderly one with more conservative ideas about the monarchy. He selected a black suit coat that went with the gray shirt he was already wearing. He knew he should add a tie, but he just couldn't do it. He was in his own home; certainly he could get away with being a little more casual there.

By the time he reached the parlor, all his instructions had been executed beautifully. Marta had placed a tray of lovely treats on the coffee table and was pouring two cups of tea. Seated on the couch was a tiny woman. Perhaps the smallest he'd ever seen, withered and hunched over with age. She was at least eighty, the life shriveling out of her just as the sun had seemed to tan her skin to near leather. Her hair was silver and pulled back into a neat bun. She looked like everyone's *abuela*.

"Presenting His Majesty, Prince Gabriel!" one of the guards lining the wall announced as he entered the room.

The old woman reached for her cane to stand and curtsey properly, but Gabriel couldn't bear for her to go to that much trouble just for him. "Please, stay seated," he insisted.

The woman relaxed back into her seat with a look of relief on her face. "*Gracias*, Don Gabriel."

He sat down opposite her, offering the woman sugar or cream for her tea. "What can I do for you, señora?"

She took a sip of tea, and then set it down on the china dish with a shaky hand. "Thank you for taking the time to see me today. I know you are very busy. My name is Conchita Ortega. In 1946 when the coup happened, I was just fifteen years old and working as a servant in the Espina household. I have seen what was published in the papers over the last week or so, and now I have heard that Señorita Espina has left Alma."

"Señorita Espina was only working for me

for a few weeks. She was always supposed to return home."

The older woman narrowed her gaze at him. "I understand, Your Grace, but I also understand and know *amor* when I see it. I know in my heart you were a couple in love and those vicious lies have ruined it. I had to speak up so you would know the truth."

Gabriel listened carefully, his interest in what the woman had to say growing with each additional word she spoke. Even though he didn't hold the past of her family against Serafia, it would help to know the truth of what really had happened back then. This woman might be one of the only people left alive who knew the whole story. "Please," he replied. "I'd love for you to tell me what you know."

She nodded and relaxed back in her seat with a cookie in her hand. She took a bite and chewed slowly, torturing Gabriel by delaying her story. "By the time everything fell apart," she began, "the hurt feelings about the broken engagement between Rafael the First and Rosa Espina were nearly a decade in the past. Rafael had married Anna Maria, Rosa had married another fine gentleman and the young Prince Rafael the Second, your grandfather, was seven years old. All had turned out for the best. The Espina family would not, and did not, conspire against the Montoros during the coup. In fact, they were your family's closest confidantes."

"How do you know?"

"At fifteen, I was like a little mouse, moving quiet and unseen through the house. I was privy to many discussions with no one giving any thought to my presence. I was serving tea when Queen Anna Maria came to the Espina Estate in secret. She'd come to ask your family to help them. Alma had weathered the Second World War, but they feared the worst was yet to come for them. Tantaberra was growing in power, staging large demonstrations and causing unrest all over Alma. The royal family was worried that they were losing hold of the country.

"The queen asked the Espinas to help them

protect Alma's historical treasures by smuggling them out of the country before things got worse. The Montoros had to stay as long as they could to appear strong against their opposition, but they feared that when they did leave, they'd have to leave everything behind. The queen couldn't bear for such important things to be lost, so they arranged for the Espinas to move to Switzerland and take the country's most important historical artifacts with them."

Serafia had mentioned that her family lived in Switzerland before moving to Spain. The article had said the family fled before the coup, which was interpreted as suspicious at the time. "What kind of things?" he asked.

"The royal jewels and stores of gold, an oil portrait of the first king of Alma, handwritten historical records of the royal family...everything that would be considered irreplaceable."

"Were they successful in smuggling everything out?" he asked.

"Yes. I helped load the ship myself. They sailed from Alma with all of their things and a secret cargo of Alman treasure. They traveled down the Rhine River to Switzerland, arriving just weeks before everything fell apart. Your family was not so lucky. They fled to America with nothing, leaving everything else behind for Tantaberra to claim as his own."

"What about you?"

"I had the option to go with the Espinas, but I couldn't leave my family behind. I stayed. But I'm glad I did so I could be here to tell you the truth. The Espinas are not traitors. They're heroes, but no one knows the truth."

"Why doesn't anyone know about this? Not even my father has mentioned it."

"It is likely he does not know. The queen orchestrated everything and may not have told anyone in the family so they could not be tortured for the information. It was a closely guarded secret and everyone was instructed not to speak of it while the Tantaberras were still in power. At the time, they had ties with Franco in Spain and they feared that if anyone knew the truth, their network would seek out the

Espinas and retaliate. They were instructed not to breathe a word to anyone until the royal family was restored officially to the throne again."

"Do you think the family still has the treasures after all these years?"

"I have no doubt of it. I ask you to reach out to Señor Espina in Madrid. He can tell you the truth. After all these years, I'm sure he will be happy to return the royal treasure to where it belongs after the coronation."

Gabriel was stunned by the entire conversation. Apparently this information had not been passed down through the generations the way it should've been. But as they finished their tea, a plan started to form in his mind. He arranged for a car to take Señora Ortega home and finalized the preparations for his flight. Instead of going to Barcelona, he decided a visit to Madrid to see Serafia's father was in order. If her family had his country's treasures, they needed to be restored to the people. Once he knew for certain the story was true, he intended for the whole country to know the truth about the Espinas. They deserved a parade in their honor, and all the vicious rumors to be put to bed once and for all.

And while he was there…he wanted to ask Señor Espina for his daughter's hand in marriage.

Twelve

It was a quick flight to Madrid, but still too long in Gabriel's eyes. The car that picked him up at the airport rushed him through the streets of the city to the Espina residence. Now all he had to do was face Serafia's father and accept his punishment for hurting her.

Arturo Espina opened the front door and glared at Gabriel. He had been expecting a less than warm reception. Serafia had no doubt told her family how horribly he'd treated her. He was on a journey to make amends not only with Serafia, but also with her parents. If what Señora Ortega said was true, things needed to be made right with the Espinas. By keeping Queen Anna Maria's secret so diligently, they'd lived in the shadow of suspicion and rumors for too long. And Gabriel had a long path to redemption where Serafia was concerned. The pain would start here, now, but it had to start somewhere.

"Señor Espina," he said, hoping his smile didn't give away how nervous he was. "Hello."

The older man glanced over Gabriel's shoulder at the royal guard hovering nearby. The irritation suddenly faded and was replaced with a respectful bow. "Prince Gabriel. To what do we owe the honor of your presence?"

"Please," Gabriel said. "You bandaged my skinned knee once. Let's drop the formalities. I'm not here as prince. I'm here about Serafia."

Arturo nodded and took a step back to allow him inside. The guard remained outside the door at Gabriel's request. Arturo led him through the large mansion to an inner courtyard landscaped with trees and a sparkling tile fountain. "Please, have a seat," he said. "May I offer you a drink? Something to eat?"

Gabriel shook his head. "No, thank you."

"I'm surprised to see you here, Gabriel. Serafia hasn't mentioned what happened in Alma, but considering how she rushed home, I'm assuming things did not end well. What I've read in the Alma newspapers has been disheartening, to say the least."

"I know, and what I'm really here to do is apologize. And maybe, if my apology is accepted, I'd like some information only you can give me."

Arturo sat down across from him and waited for the questions to come.

"First, I want to apologize for the way I've handled all this. Regardless of the truth, I behaved poorly, lashing out at Serafia, and I'm ashamed of that. Your family, and specifically your daughter, never gave me any reason to doubt your loyalty."

"You are not the first to be suspicious of our family over the years."

"I had never heard any of those stories before," Gabriel explained. "The papers have had some terrible things to say about your family. I grew up in America in a household that very rarely, if ever, discussed Alma and what happened. Our families have always been friends, so I was blindsided by those stories. I feel like a fool, but I allowed those articles to taint my feelings for your family and for your daughter. I shouldn't have let that happen, but I was upset with myself and took it out on her."

"I read about what happened at the oil rig. Am I wrong in thinking that was related to your abduction?"

Gabriel looked Arturo in the eye. "It was. I wasn't sure how many people knew about it. My father wanted to keep it all pretty quiet."

"He called me while it was happening and asked for advice. Rafael was torn up about the whole thing and how it was taking so long to bring you home. Rafael was so frustrated—he felt helpless for the first time in his life. When you showed back up in Miami, I think he was embarrassed about how it was all handled and never wanted to talk about it again. He thought you would blame him for everything, so he wanted to forget about it all."

"I didn't blame him," Gabriel said. "But I've always felt like I was a disappointment to him, somehow. I tried to hide my claustrophobia because I thought he'd see it as another weakness."

"No one—your father included—would hold something like that against you. You went through a terrible experience. He probably thought that putting it behind you would help. We did that with Serafia and I've never been certain it was the right course. But as parents, you do what you can to protect your children."

Gabriel sighed. He'd come here for answers about the Espina family and ended up with more than he'd expected. "Thank you for telling me that. I've never really been able to get past what happened. I don't do well in small spaces since my kidnapping, and I blamed Serafia for not warning me ahead of time about what was in store on the oil rig. It wasn't her fault. I ruined everything with her, and then I find out that all those rumors that poisoned my mind weren't even true."

"Do you mean the rumors about the Espinas helping Tantaberra depose your family?" Arturo asked. His tone was flat, as though he'd had to hear these slanderous charges his whole life.

"Yes. An old woman who worked for your family back then came to the house today and explained the truth about how the Espinas safeguarded the royal treasure. At least, I hope it's the truth."

Arturo nodded. "We've had to keep quiet about our family's role in all this for decades, ignoring the rumors so we didn't risk anyone finding out the truth. I don't think any of them believed the dictatorship would last as long as it has. We feared that the Tantaberras would come after us if they knew what we were hiding, or worse, come after your family if they had any knowledge of it. Even after all this time, we had to deliberately keep it from you and others in your family."

"I can't imagine that burden."

"I think it was worth it. I heard that Tanta-berra was furious when he took the palace and all the gold and jewels he'd coveted were gone."

Gabriel had never given much thought to his great-grandmother, Anna Maria, but in that moment, he admired her fire. He wished he could've seen the dictator's face when he realized that the Montoros had outsmarted him. "That means your family still has it?"

Arturo stood. "Wait here. I'll be right back." He disappeared down a hallway and returned a few minutes later with something in his hand. When he sat down again, he placed two small items on the table. One, a gold coin, and the other, a diamond and ruby ring. "This is just a small part of what my family has protected for seventy years."

Gabriel reached out and picked up the coin. It was a coin minted in Alma in the 1800s. "You keep it here?"

"No. I've always kept a few tiny items in my safe for a moment like this, but the rest is in a vault in Switzerland. We were to keep it until the coronation took place, to ensure it was official, and then it can all be restored to the palace. I've always hoped to see this day happen. It's been a weight on my shoulders since my father told me the truth."

Returning the coin, Gabriel examined the ruby ring and felt a touch of sadness come over him. It was so beautiful, with a dark red oval ruby that had to be nearly four carats. It was surrounded by a ring of tiny diamonds and flanked on each side by a pear-shaped diamond. The setting was a mix of platinum and gold filigree. It was more beautiful than any ring had a right to be. He was incredibly grateful the Espinas had hidden it away from the Tantaberras, yet sad that no one had enjoyed the ring for all these years. This ring was meant to be on the hand of a queen—a woman like Serafia.

"I've betrayed the family that I should've trusted above all others. I'm so sorry. I can't apologize enough. I want to see to it that the truth gets out. When the treasure is restored,

I want it put on display in Alma's national museum so that everyone will know how the Espinas safeguarded it all these years, and put an end to the rumors once and for all."

"That would be wonderful," Arturo said. "I would like to move back to Alma one day. My father was born there. I grew up in Switzerland, but I've always dreamed of going back to where my people belonged."

Looking down at the ring, Gabriel was reminded of the other reason he'd come here today. The truth was nice, but even if the old woman's story was just a fabrication, his first priority was getting Serafia to forgive—and marry—him. He put the ring back on the table and looked at Arturo.

"I also came here today because I want Serafia in my life," he said. "I...I love her. I want her to be my queen. Do you think she'll ever be able to forgive me for the way I've treated her?"

Arturo sat back in his seat and looked at him with a serious expression. "I don't know. She's taken this very hard. Her mother and I have been worried about her."

Gabriel's gaze met his. "Worried?"

"Did she tell you about her illness?" Arturo asked.

"The anorexia? Yes, but she said that was behind her."

"We'd hoped so," Arturo explained, "but her doctors had warned us that patients are never fully cured of this disease. Stress, especially emotional upheaval, can send her spiraling back into her bad habits. Her housekeeper has told us that she is hardly eating. That she does nothing but exercise and sleep since she returned to Barcelona. There have been a few times where she's fallen into this slump before, but she's righted herself before it went too far. I'm hoping that you can help pull her out of it."

Gabriel sensed the worry and fear in Arturo's voice and felt even more miserable than he had before. He knew how much Serafia struggled with her image and how hard she'd worked to overcome her illness. She'd done so well when they were together that he never would've known about the anorexia if she hadn't told him the truth. If he'd sent her into such an emotional state that she fell prey to it again—if she got hurt because of it—he'd never forgive himself.

"I'm flying directly to Barcelona from here. I'll do everything I can to make things right, I promise. Even if she doesn't want me, even if she won't forgive me, I won't leave until I'm certain she's safe."

Arturo watched him as he spoke, and then nodded. "You said earlier that you wanted my daughter to be your queen. You're serious about this?"

Gabriel swallowed hard. "Yes, sir. With your permission, I'd like to ask Serafia to be my wife. I know that under the circumstances, the public role will not be an easy one for her, but I love her too much to let her out of my life. I don't think I could choose a better woman to help me make Alma that great country it once was."

Arturo nodded. "You are good for her, I know

it. I've watched you two on the news together. She looks happier with you than she has been in years. You make sure she stays that way and you have my blessing."

"Yes. Of course. I only want Serafia to be happy. Thank you, Señor Espina."

Serafia's father finally smiled for the first time since Gabriel had arrived, and he felt a weight lifted from his chest.

"Do you have a ring for her?" the older man asked.

Gabriel was embarrassed to admit that he didn't. "I rushed here to see you without thinking all of it through. I don't have anything for her yet."

Arturo reached out and picked up the ruby ring from the table. "This is the wedding ring of Rafael the First's mother, Queen Josefina. If you truly love my daughter and want her to be queen, this is the ring you should give her."

Gabriel took the ring from the man who might soon be his father-in-law and shook his hand. "Thank you, sir. It's perfect."

* * *

"Good job," Esperanza said as she took away Serafia's mostly empty dinner plate.

Serafia chuckled. "Does this mean I get the tiramisu you promised me?"

"Of course."

Esperanza disappeared inside, leaving her alone on her patio, watching the sun set. It seemed like only yesterday that she was doing the same with Gabriel, only overlooking the Atlantic instead of the Mediterranean. The moment had been romantic and full of promise.

And now here she was, alone. What a difference a few days could make.

But she wasn't going to dwell on it. She'd had her moment to mope, and now it was time for her to figure out what she wanted to do with her life. Being with Gabriel had helped her realize that she was hiding here in Barcelona. She got out, she worked, but she hadn't really allowed herself to have the full life she deserved. That was over. She was determined that from this point forward, she was going to live her life to the fullest.

"Señorita?" Esperanza was at the door again.

"Yes?" Serafia said as she turned and froze in place. Standing tall behind her tiny housekeeper was Gabriel. He was looking incredibly handsome in a gray shirt and a black suit coat. Without a tie, of course.

She felt her heart skip a beat in her chest when she saw him. Every nerve awakened as her body realized he was so close. She tightened her hands around the arms of her chair to fight her unwanted reaction to him. He was a bastard. He said terrible things to her. She absolutely should not react to him like this. And yet she couldn't help it. He might be a bastard, but she still loved him. She still hadn't managed to convince her heart differently.

Taking a deep breath, she wished away her attraction and tried to focus on more important things, like what had brought him all the way to her doorstep.

Esperanza looked a little stunned. Serafia

imagined that opening the door and finding a prince standing there was not exactly what the older woman had anticipated when the bell rang. "Prince Gabriel is here to see you. He would not wait outside."

"I didn't want to give you the chance to turn me away," he said, with a sheepish smile that seemed to acknowledge he was the guilty party.

"Smart move," Serafia noted in a sharp tone. He *was* the guilty party and she wanted to make sure he got his punishment. "Esperanza, could you please bring out a bottle of merlot and two glasses, please?" She wasn't sure how this conversation was going to go, but drinking certainly wouldn't hurt matters. At the very least it would help her relax. She was drawn tight as a drum.

Esperanza disappeared into the house and Gabriel joined Serafia outside. He took a seat in the chair beside her and looked out at the sea as she had been doing earlier.

"You have a beautiful home," he said.

"Thank you."

He turned back to look at her, his concerned gaze taking in every inch of her, but not in the hungry way she was used to. He seemed to be cataloguing her somehow. "How are you?" he asked.

Not once in the weeks they'd spent together had he asked her that question. Now she knew it was probably her parents' doing. They'd started calling each day, never directly asking if she was eating, but hinting around the subject, not knowing Esperanza had already ratted them out. She frowned at him. "Did my family send you down here to check on me?"

"What?" He looked startled. "No. I came here on my own, but I made a stop in Madrid on the way. Your father mentioned they were concerned about you."

"They usually are," she said. "That's why I opted to move to Barcelona and give myself some breathing room. They're very overprotective of me."

"They just want to make sure you're happy and healthy. As do I."

"Is that why you've come?" she snapped. "To make sure you didn't break my heart too badly?"

"No," he said with a grave seriousness in his voice. "I came to apologize."

"It's not necessary," she said.

"Yes, it is. I lashed out at you and it wasn't your fault. I let my own fears get the best of me, then used the most convenient excuse I could find to push you away. It was the dumbest thing I've ever done, and that's saying a lot after the antics I've gotten into the last few years. I've relived that moment in my head over and over, wishing I'd handled everything differently. I was a fool and it cost me the woman I love."

Serafia gasped at his words, but before she could respond, Esperanza returned with the wine. The interruption allowed Serafia a minute to think about his words and consider what her response should be. He loved her. She wanted to tell him that she loved him, too, but she was wary of giving away too much. He'd hurt her, abused her trust. She wasn't just going to take

ANDREA LAURENCE   281

him back because he decided he was in love
and that made everything better.

When Esperanza went back into the house, he
picked up where he'd left off. "I never believed
those stories about your family, and now that I
know the truth, I'm going to see to it that those
rumors are put to bed for good. The Espinas are
heroes and I want everyone to know it."

"Heroes?" Serafia frowned. What was he
talking about?

"Your family protected the royal treasure
from the Tantaberras. That's why they left before the coup. Your father and I are going to
work to have the treasure restored and put on
display after the coronation. Without your family's help, the Tantaberras would've used up and
destroyed our country's history."

Serafia had never heard any of this before,
but she didn't doubt the truth of it. Her father
had made more than a few mysterious trips to
Switzerland over the years. At the same time,
the truth didn't make everything okay, either.

"So now that you know I don't come from a line of traitors, you've decided you can love me?"

"No. Stop jumping to these horrible conclusions. I'm happy I found out the truth, but no, that's got nothing to do with why I'm here. I had one foot out the door to come see you when all this fell into my lap. But in the end, none of it has to do with us. That's all in the past. What I'm interested in is you and me and the future."

Serafia's breath caught in her throat. She reached a shaky hand out for her wine, hoping it would steady her, but all she could do was hold the glass as he continued to speak.

"I love you, Serafia, with all my heart and all my soul. I am a fool and I don't deserve your love in return, but if someday I could earn it back, I would be the happiest man in the world." Gabriel reached out and took her hand and she was too stunned to pull away.

"I don't just love you. I don't just want you to come back to Alma. I went to Madrid because I wanted to ask your father for his blessing to marry you. I want you to be my queen."

Gabriel slipped out of his chair and onto one knee. Serafia sat stunned as she watched him reach into his inner breast pocket. She saw a momentary flash of gold and realized he was wearing the pocket watch she gave him, but then he pulled out a small ring box and her thoughts completely disintegrated into incoherence.

"I don't know if I'm the right man to be king. But fate has put the crown in my hands and because of you, I feel like I'm closer than I could ever be to the kind of man my people deserve. With you by my side as queen, all my doubts are gone. We can restore Alma to its former glory together. I don't think Alma could ask for a better queen and I couldn't ask for a smarter, more beautiful, graceful and caring bride. Would you do me the honor of being my wife?"

Gabriel opened the box and stunned her with an amazing bloodred ruby with diamonds. It was unlike any ring she'd ever seen before. It was the kind of ring that was fit for royalty.

"This ring belonged to my great-great-grandmother, Queen Josefina. It was her wedding ring and part of the treasure entrusted to your family to protect. Your father returned it to me today. He told me that it belonged on your finger and I quite agree."

Serafia let him slip the ring onto her finger. She couldn't take her eyes off it and couldn't stop thinking about everything it represented. He loved her. He wanted to marry her. He wanted her to be his queen. In that moment, all her doubts and hesitations about being in the spotlight disappeared. Before, she had been there alone. If Gabriel was by her side, it would okay. She couldn't believe how quickly everything in her life had changed.

"Serafia?"

She tore her gaze away from the ring to look at Gabriel. He looked a little confused and a little anxious as he watched her. "Yes?"

"I, uh, asked you a question. Would you like to answer it so I can stop freaking out?"

Serafia smiled, feeling quite silly for missing

the critical step in the proposal process. "Yes, Gabriel, I will marry you."

He grinned wide, opening his arms to catch her just as she propelled herself at him. Her lips met his with an enthusiasm she couldn't contain. Just an hour ago, she thought she might never be in his arms again. And here she was… his fiancée. There was a sudden lightness in her heart and she felt as though she had to cling to Gabriel so she wouldn't float away.

"I love you, Serafia," he whispered against her lips.

"I love you, too, Gabriel," she answered, happy to finally say those words out loud.

Gabriel stood up, pulling her up with him. "The coronation is over a month away. I don't want to wait that long to marry you."

She knew exactly how he felt. She would happily elope if she thought they would get away with it. Unfortunately the people of Alma would want their royal wedding. As would her mother. There was no avoiding that. "How quickly do you think we can pull off a wedding?"

"Well," Gabriel said thoughtfully, "my brother's wedding is already in the works. He abdicated, but he's still prince, so father insisted he and Emily have their ceremony in Alma. That's only a few weeks away. What would you say to a double wedding?"

"A double wedding?"

"Why not? They've already got the plans in place. All the same people will be coming. Why can't we have one giant celebration and both marry at the same time?"

Serafia looked at her handsome fiancé thoughtfully. He was not a woman. He didn't understand what kinds of expectations went into a wedding. Serafia might not mind a double wedding, but Emily certainly might.

"How about this…?" she proposed. "You talk to Rafe and Emily about it. If they are both fine with it, then I'm okay with it, too."

Gabriel grinned wide. "I'm sure they will be, but I'll check. And then you'll be Mrs. Gabriel Montoro, soon to be *Su Majestad la Reina Serafia de Alma*. Are you ready for that?"

Serafia wrapped her arms around his neck and nodded. "I think so, although I'm sure that being queen will be the easy part."

Gabriel arched one brow curiously at her. "What's going to be the hard part?"

She climbed to her bare toes and planted a kiss on his full lips. "Keeping the king out of trouble."

* * * * *

MILLS & BOON®

Why shop at millsandboon.co.uk?

Each year, thousands of romance readers find their perfect read at millsandboon.co.uk. That's because we're passionate about bringing you the very best romantic fiction. Here are some of the advantages of shopping at www.millsandboon.co.uk:

* **Get new books first**—you'll be able to buy your favourite books one month before they hit the shops

* **Get exclusive discounts**—you'll also be able to buy our specially created monthly collections, with up to 50% off the RRP

* **Find your favourite authors**—latest news, interviews and new releases for all your favourite authors and series on our website, plus ideas for what to try next

* **Join in**—once you've bought your favourite books, don't forget to register with us to rate, review and join in the discussions

Visit **www.millsandboon.co.uk**
for all this and more today!